LOVE IS MURDER

C.H. LYN, TRACEY BARSKI

To all the besties out there, this one is for you.

CONTENTS

PROLOGUE OF MURDER

I followed at a distance, my eyes trained intently on the figure ahead of me. He walked as if he had nothing to worry about. It was that asshole swagger of an over-inflated ego, so sure he could never be anyone's target. Every step on the pavement moved rhythmically, his gait announcing his douchebagery to the world.

I amused myself by filling the word in time with each of his steps: *douche-bag, douche-bag, douche-bag.*

I tipped my head back and forth as if it were the beat to a song, a theme for trash human beings everywhere.

Keep walking. Keep that beat so I can count myself in for my solo.

I wouldn't claim that it gave me any sort of thrill when I called his name softly and his mouth curved up at the sight of me. Or when his brows crashed over his eyes in confusion when my knife slid so smoothly into those obsessively cultivated washboard abs of his.

No, the thrill came from knowing he couldn't hurt anyone else again, that I was taking out some particularly fetid sewage and leaving it for the garbage truck to pick up in the morning.

It was quick work late at night on an empty street. The location was not one that would make him think twice about being followed or induce anyone to check for evidence of a brutal crime.

Plus, I always came prepared. Thank you, *Glad,* for providing the stretchiest and most obnoxiously perfumed trash bags for my less-than-wholesome side gig. They might be more expensive, but nothing contained long-limbed, self-obsessed victimizers quite like these bags.

And I was secure in knowing I could drag this trash bag of douchebag to the curb with the rest of this house's garbage cans without leaving a trail of innards. We'd all seen the commercials, and they weren't lying, even if leftover lasagna didn't quite compare to human bodily fluids. Durable plastic was durable plastic.

I situated the bag against the cans, checking my watch for the time. I knew this neighborhood had early pickup. Usually before most people headed out to work. I was nothing but thorough when it came to research, and I'd picked this neighborhood for a reason. It was convenient that this guy was predictable.

All it took was a strategic message, an alluring enough photo for this sicko to come running. And it confirmed what I'd already suspected then uncovered about him.

So, no. I got no shot of excitement. It wasn't joy. It was no drug to my system. Because I wasn't some psycho.

But there was a satisfaction in knowing I'd done the world some good.

Even if I got blood on my lucky sweater. Again.

CHAPTER ONE

NIGHT CLUB VS BOOK CLUB

"You promised," I mutter through gritted teeth as Zoe asks—again—if we can just ditch this line and go home.

"I didn't know we'd be standing here for an hour before we even get in."

My lip curls as I glare at my best friend. "It's a club. That's how clubs work. Don't pretend you didn't know this."

Zoe plants a hand on her hip, a feat given the size of the bag she's chosen to bring. I switch tactics.

"One night a month, Zoe, that's all I'm asking. A new city and a fresh start doesn't mean much if we never meet anyone new."

"I don't want to meet anyone new."

I roll my eyes and adjust the sheer black lace covering my tank top. This outfit is as new as we are, fresh from my new job at a boutique downtown, fresh as the apartment we just finished deep cleaning, fresh as the hurt still thudding through my stomach each time I check my phone and see a blank screen.

"Karrie."

I jolt from spacing at the screen. Zoe has a gentle grip on my arm, tugging me forward as we finally reach the front of the line.

"Sorry." I flash a grin and tuck the phone back into my high-waisted pants pocket. *I* didn't bring a bag to the club because *I'm* not a crazy person.

"Nothing back?" Zoe runs her hand up and down my arm in a comforting gesture, immaculate Barbie-pink nails a major contrast to my darker tones.

"No, but you know guys and that dumb three day rule. I'm sure he'll call me tomorrow." I run a hand through my carefully curled hair and shake off the frustration bubbling within. Tonight isn't about a guy I've been on two dates with. Tonight is about meeting people, dancing, and having fun.

The bouncer waves us through, giving Zoe a wink that she replies to with a sneer. I stifle my giggle as we find a spot at the bar and settle in to get some drinks.

"How about you?" I ask, slurping a bright blue icy drink through a twisty straw. "How's work been going?"

Zoe shrugs a slender shoulder beneath her fuzzy pink sweater. "HR wasn't happy about the switch to remote, but I'm loving it."

"School?" I quickly approach the end of my drink, the gurgling sound of straw meeting empty cup filling the space between us.

"Classes don't start for another few weeks."

"Perfect," I give her a wicked grin, "just enough time for us to find some friends and explore the city."

Her brilliant blue eyes go wide with mild panic.

"Kidding, I'm kidding." I heave a sigh. "I'll find *me* some friends. But you're exploring the city with me. Non-negotiable."

Her jaw juts to the side in a stubborn look I've known since we were both too young to drive.

I wait. And wait. And slurp my straw some more until the gurgling noise makes her wince, and she nods.

"Fine! Fine, we can try something new…"

"Once a week."

She opens her mouth, ready to object, but I cut her off.

"Once a week for plain old exploring. I'll keep social places limited to once a month."

Zoe stares at me for a long moment. Then she heaves a sigh. "Deal."

I scoot off my barstool, give her a peck on the cheek, and then abandon her for the dance floor. I know better than to ask if she wants to join me. Zoe dances, but at very specific times and places: namely alone in the middle of the night in our living room.

I prefer the middle of the dance floor, my arms in the air, spinning to a weird reverb remix of W.I.T.C.H. After a handful of songs, and a handful of numbers exchanged with potential friends and two cute guys, I return to the bar for a water.

I fight and lose against the urge to roll my eyes. "Zoe!"

She raises her eyes from the depths of the chunky *book* she brought to a nightclub. A book. To a nightclub.

"What are you doing?" My tone is dry as I plant my hands on my hips.

She blinks in utter innocence. "Reading."

I heave a sigh. "Please stop bringing books to clubs."

"Please stop bringing *me* to clubs," she replies, the hint of an exasperated smile behind the thin line her lips make.

I flop down beside her. "Zoe, you're stunning."

Her mouth twitches at the corners. "Accurate."

"You could get any guy in here." I swing my arm wide to encompass the whole room.

She looks at the dance floor, then back to me, no change in her bored expression. "I don't want a guy."

I roll my eyes. "Any girl then."

"Them either."

"Fine then," I say through gritted teeth. "Live alone with a cat."

Zoe meets my eye, a twinkle of delight at my irritation glinting in those baby blues. "I do like cats."

"You're impossible." I chug a glass of water.

"Someone left this for you, by the way." She hands me a slip of paper with a phone number and no name.

"Who?" I glance around, checking out a few of the cuter guys to see if any make prolonged eye contact.

"I don't know." She scoffs. "Some freckly dude."

"Right." I tuck the paper into my back pocket, thinking it must be that guy who asked me to dance. I politely declined, but it's not the worst thing to have a back-up number just in case. I finish off my water and leave her to the book, choosing to get my cardio in for the week on the dance floor.

CHAPTER TWO

GHOST TOWN

Deep diving into someone's life is really no different than doing research for my thesis. In fact, it plays to that part of my brain that just *has* to know every nano-detail about something that interests me.

Or triggers my suspicion. Which really are two sides of the same coin.

Trashbag Douchebag had been a walking red flag. Which, honestly, still baffles me because Karrie didn't see it. Not that she often sees past six-pack abs and a chiseled face.

Objectively, he was a good-looking dude by society's standards. It triggered literally nothing in me, but I know what beauty is in the abstract.

Karrie, for example, is drop-dead gorgeous. And she'd prefer that exact descriptor since her style borders on glam-goth. Her dark hair is shiny and thick; her face is a perfectly symmetrical heart shape with large, dark eyes that seem to lure in a mind-boggling number of men. Plus, she has a killer bod.

Again, this is objective observation, and I can appreciate Karrie's flagrant disregard for societal standards as far as virtue is concerned. Girl can do whatever—and whoever—she wants, and I'll maim anyone who comes at her for it, though I don't understand her inclination in the slightest.

We'd long come to the conclusion that there was nothing inside of me that called for something from anyone else. Which was a damn shame, given that I, objectively speaking, am also a sight to behold. If Baywatch were still a thing, I'd probably have a good shot at scoring the role of stacked blonde bimbo, despite having an IQ of somewhere in the 140s and a deep abhorrence for the ocean.

Alas, the only person I really love is myself—aside from my strictly platonic but undying devotion to Karrie. It's been a regular disappointment to both my best friend and my mother that I can find no spark in myself for any man *or* woman. The closest I come is my deep and abiding love for the color pink.

And cyber dirt-digging.

But hey, look at me! I'm more multifaceted than I give myself credit for.

I check the clock on the stove and click out of the news articles I've been perusing in order to bring up the boring work reports I'm supposed to be focusing on. It's only two minutes before the deadbolt unlocks from the outside.

Karrie breezes in, her brows furrowed and her shoulders slumped as she kicks off her black combat boots.

She almost leaves them right there in front of the door until she sees my pointed look, then she sheepishly bends down to pick them up and sets them neatly on the shoe rack I specifically measured so that it would fit perfectly between the TV stand and the front door.

With exaggerated movements, she hangs her jacket on one of the hooks I also painstakingly measured and positioned and sets her purse strap over it, leaving the floor perfectly clear—exactly how I like it. I don't even care that she is clearly silently cursing me while doing it.

Then she theatrically throws herself onto the couch next to my desk and releases the most long-suffering exhale I've ever heard. Well, we'd been friends since toddler-hood, so I'd probably heard the same sound a million times because it's a Karrie staple. But it's the first time *today*, and I know it's to pull me into question mode.

I'm glad to play along because, you know, undying platonic devotion. Not to mention I have a pretty solid guess as to what she's frustrated about, and it's imperative that I ask about it in earnest innocence.

"What's the problem, Kar?"

She gives a very feminine growl. "That guy, Derek—remember from the other night? He totally ghosted me!"

I make a point to widen my eyes and gasp. "What an asshole!"

She grimaces and tips her head back. "I mean, we really hit it off. I thought for *sure* after the dumb dude rule about waiting three days or whatever, he'd call me." She suddenly lurches forward, narrowing her dark eyes on my face.

I freeze, thinking she finally has me figured.

"Am I too clingy?" She stares at me like my face is a particularly difficult math equation. Which she would know because she's a brilliant mathematician. No one would ever guess given that she never finished college, works in a fashion boutique downtown, and goes out partying most weekends.

I snort, a flood of relief filling my chest. "You're like the least clingy woman I've ever met."

She rolls her eyes. "You have met yourself, right?"

"I don't recall ever meeting myself, no."

"Zoe!"

I hold up my hands. "Karrie, you're smart, beautiful, probably an excellent kisser based on the noises these dudes make when you make out with them in your room, you've got the ass of a goddess, and you're the perfect balance of sexy and cool. You are not too clingy." *You just have shit taste in men*, I silently add.

"Then why does this always happen to me?" She throws herself back against the cushions. "I'm cursed!"

More like indiscriminate, but I let it pass.

I lift a shoulder. "Listen, he just isn't the guy for you. He was a fun fling. It's not like you're looking to get married or something." I turn back to my computer, very deliberately trying to look like I'm shutting down something I had absolutely been in the middle of.

She purses her lips, glaring at the TV when I glance at her from the corner of my eye. "What if I am looking to get married?"

I spin back around, slapping my hands on my lap. "If that guy is in the running, then your prospects for a happy life are very dismal."

She pouts. "You just hate the idea of marriage."

I lean forward, forcing her to make eye contact with me. "For me. I am not interested in marrying anyone ever. It's been established." I take her hand. "But *you* would make a lovely bride, but only for a deserving guy. I'll be damned if I never get to be your maid of honor. You know exactly what color I'm picking for the dresses."

She makes an unattractive sound in the back of her throat. "It's *my* wedding. I'm supposed to pick the color of the bridesmaid dresses."

I just give her a blank stare.

"Fine!" She throws her arms into the air.

"I can't let you put us all in black. It would be a travesty with my complexion."

She mutters something about leopard print and snatches the remote off the arm of the couch, punching the *on* button with more force than necessary, but I simply stand up to get some kind of dinner going instead of scolding her.

I step into the kitchen when the news anchor's voice rings out in that robotic cadence that always sounds so false to me.

"*...missing man, Derek Waters, who was last seen by coworkers six days ago.*"

I freeze, my eyes shooting straight to Karrie's horrified face as it drains of all color. "Oh, my God. Zoe."

My heart beat picks up, and my fingers curl into my palms. Oxygen momentarily becomes scarce. It takes me way too long to realize she's not accusing me of anything.

"*An investigation into his disappearance has led police to a cache of child pornography and other evidence of deviant behavior—*"

She punches the mute button, her wide eyes shifting to me. "Oh, my God. Zoe!" she repeats. "It happened again! I really *am* cursed."

Sure, cursed with terrible taste in men, I want to say. Because, you know, kiddie porn. Even if she was aware that he wasn't marriage material, she didn't have the where-withal to know that he was definitely not temporary bang material either.

But if I say any of that, I'm sure I'll sound suspicious. Maybe. Wait, no. There's no reason Karrie would suspect me of having a hand in any of it. Because why would she? Better to be on the safe side, though, and keep my mouth shut.

Karrie shoots to her feet and begins pacing. "I bet the cops are going to come here. They'll want to know about our date. Oh, God! What if I was the last to see him alive?"

I walk a little further into the room, trying not to fiddle with the hem of my sweater. "What makes you think he's dead?"

Karrie stops pacing and looks at me. "Oh. You're right." She puts a hand to her mouth, delicate brows furrowing. "I'm jumping to conclusions."

"They will probably want to talk to you though," I say, unhelpfully. "But we both know you had nothing to do with it, so no problem." I shrug, forcing the panic out of my own body by sheer force of will.

It isn't likely they'll think I had anything to do with it either, so I don't need to worry too much. I'm a little annoyed that this will get linked back to Karrie so quickly though.

She sinks down on the couch. "I can't believe this is happening to me again."

"We'll get through it, Kar." I go all the way into the kitchen. "Mac and cheese sound good?"

She makes a noncommittal sound that I take as a yes, and I search for something neutral to talk about while I set to work making gourmet mac and cheese—at least my version of it. I usually add seasoned chicken and the fancy cheeses.

"Hey, when you get off tomorrow, do you mind picking up my sweater from the dry-cleaner's?"

"What sweater?" Her voice is still dejected.

"My lucky sweater." I pour myself a glass of wine, fully acknowledging to myself it's a prop.

"Wait, why is it at the cleaner's again? You never go anywhere; why do you keep having to dry-clean this sweater?""

I walk back out to the living room, giving her a benign smile, though she's glaring at me suspiciously. "It had a wine stain."

She narrows her eyes even further. "Which one is your lucky sweater?"

"You know. The pink fuzzy one." I take a sip. Cool, casual. Keep eye contact.

"All of your sweaters are pink." She gestures at me to prove her point, as I'm clad in hot pink wool today. "It must not be very lucky if you keep spilling on it."

More like *keep killing on it.*

I almost choke on my sip of wine at my own joke, and it's one of the few times I wish she knew my little secret so I could share my jokes with her.

She probably wouldn't think they were funny, though. Murder isn't supposed to be.

Chapter Three

A Tale of Two Dates

Customer service is one of the top most-hated jobs in America. I'll be honest, I just don't get it. I've loved it since I was fifteen and working my first hostess job at a shitty diner. It's even better now.

I dance through the doors to the petite boutique I've been working at for the past month since the move. Didn't take long to get the gig; my resume is stacked with stuff like this. Besides, Catherine, the owner of Bound by Fashion, is a sweetheart. The kind of lady who doesn't mind me wearing four-inch platform boots with my fishnets. The kind who doesn't throw a fit over heavy dark make-up and skull earrings.

"Hey!" I stuff my purse under the counter and duck my head into the back office to let Catherine know I made it. "Thanks for understanding the delay."

The owner, a stout woman with bright red hair and impeccable taste in outfits, looks up from paperwork with a sympathetic expression. "Of course. How'd it go?"

I lift and drop a shoulder. There's no good way to answer that. I spent the morning being questioned by cops about Derek Waters. I had to field questions like, *When did you last see him? How many dates did you go on?* and *Did you know about his collection of kiddie porn?*

Cue about a thousand groans and a headache from how hard I was cringing. They kicked me to the curb pretty quickly. No reason to keep a two-date bimbo around—or so said one of the cops when they thought I couldn't hear them.

My concerns about being cursed weren't brought up. Why? Because I only need one person in my life thinking I'm crazy.

The questioning went well because I'm not a suspect in his disappearance. It went well because the lady cop was nice and complimented my necklace. It went well because the cop shop is next to an awesome donut place, and I've got a caffeine and sugar buzz going that'll get me through a slow Tuesday afternoon.

It sucked because Derek Waters is about the dozenth guy I've dated in the last several years to completely ghost me, and the third to go missing.

That little tidbit didn't make it to the cops.

"It went well," I say to Catherine. "I only went on two dates with the guy, thank god."

She nods fervently.

I head to the front, organizing a few clothing racks, folding up some cute graphic Tees, and helping an older woman find a new fashion sense after a rough divorce. She's grateful, changing into one of her hot outfits before she even leaves.

I'm happy to help her and bummed to hear that none of her friends had any interest in joining her for a rebranding of her style. Zoe has always been Miss Pink, but I've gone through a hundred phases since we were teenagers.

I shudder at a memory of cowgirl boots that gave me blisters for weeks.

I hit a smoothie shop down the street for my late lunch break. A freckled man with dark hair cut in a low fade sits on the far end of the bar munching his bagel.

I slurp a blueberry blackberry swirl, hoping it'll make my teeth purple, and scroll through a dating app for a few minutes before shoving it into my pocket with a sigh.

Maybe I should take a break from the dating life for a bit. Derek was the first guy I met out here and look what happened.

The thought has barely crossed my mind when a small group of guys pushes through the doors.

Chiseled is the first adjective that comes to mind. Followed closely by my wondering how these men would look done up. They're clearly fresh from the gym, the loose tanks emphasizing biceps that need no extra help.

I swallow a mouthful of smoothie and try not to drool.

The three of them order, and then the blond one mutters something to his friends and crosses the room towards me.

I straighten, not needing to with the cut of this shirt, but I know what it does for my boobs when I utilize good posture.

"Hi," I say before his mouth opens.

There's a brief pause; he wasn't expecting me to speak first. Then he recovers and flashes a dazzling smile. Those teeth had braces and probably whiteners every few months. No way they're naturally that straight.

"Hey."

Oh that's a deep voice. My heartbeat quickens.

"I haven't seen you in here before." He leans against the hightop counter I'm sitting at.

It's a lame line, but he's cute. "I'm new to town," I reply.

"Then this is perfect." He grins. "I know all the best places. I can show you around."

I give my lower lip the slightest bite, just enough to catch his gaze and bring a hitch to his breathing.

With a grin, I nod. "That sounds fun. I get off work at eight."

There it is again, that widening of his eyes at my forwardness. It's kinda cute.

"Awesome." He stands for a moment, seeming unsure of the next step.

"I'm Karrie." I extend a hand and a lifeline.

He takes it. "Trent."

"Well, Trent, where can I meet you?"

He gives me the name of a tapas restaurant not far from here, and we agree to meet up at nine. Gives me plenty of time to run home, change, and put on a fresh coat of purple glitter eyeshadow.

I leave before Trent and his friends, flouncing out the door with heightened awareness that they're getting a show as I walk away. Not a problem. I'm expecting to find out if Trent's abs match his biceps in the next couple weeks. Hell, tonight if things go well.

I shoot off a quick text to let Zoe know I'll be in and out tonight. She responds with an eye-roll emoji that pulls a chuckle from me. I send a picture of her lucky sweater hanging in the back of the car and a tongue sticking out.

She sends a black heart.

The rest of the day flies by. I'm organizing a row of belts so I can lock up when the little bell above the door dings.

"Welcome to Bound!" I holler toward the front in my sweetest customer service voice. "We close in ten minutes, but feel free to look around until then."

There's a muffled response. I pop my head around a stand of watches and wallets.

"Oh," I murmur before catching myself.

A brief flash of regret about my date tonight tightens my stomach, but I shake it off.

The man stepping up to the empty check-out counter is tall. He's of Asian descent, with dark angular brows and warm creamy brown skin. Nearly as tall as Zoe, I'm briefly distracted by wondering if he's as dark under the neat collar of his button-up.He's gone for business casual—dark jeans, clean shave, and a tucked-in shirt.

"Hey there." He turns at the sight of me, skipping the counter and walking my way. "You don't happen to be Karrie Dunshire, do you?"

"In the flesh." I raise an eyebrow. "What can I do for ya?"

He offers up a crooked smile, not the dazzling display Trent had, but certainly nothing unpleasant to look at. "I was hoping I could ask you some questions."

My smile falters, the words reminding me of the cops this morning. "About what?"

"Well..." His hesitation is just about all I need to know what's coming next. "Uh, you have... that is to say... Jeez, I'm not sure how to put this without sounding awful."

"Just spit it out." My voice is monotone.

He gives a sharp nod. "You have a track record of men disappearing after they date you."

My mouth goes dry. I chew on my inner lip, frustration bubbling up through me. "Well, I certainly get ghosted plenty. I don't know what constitutes a 'track record'."

He looks thoughtful and pulls a small notebook from a back pocket. "I've got a total of six names of guys who went missing after they dated you."

Surprise widens my eyes, and I move toward him. "What?"

He glances at me. "You didn't know?"

"I know I can't get a text back to save my life, but I didn't know that many of them were actually, like, legit missing."

He flips open his notebook and sets it on the counter for me to look at. I recognize most of the names. That guy on our trip to Toronto must have given me a fake because I recognize the scribbled description, but not the name beside it.

"What the actual fuck..." I breathe. My hands are trembling. Suspicion leaps to the front of my brain. "Who are you? What is this?"

"Sorry." He chuckles awkwardly. "I'm the Armchair Detective."

I squint at him. "What?"

"Uh, well my name is Zack, Zack Lim, but I run a podcast called the Armchair Detective."

"You're a detective?

He grimaces. "Not officially, not with the police or anything. It's just what I call the podcast. Sort of to keep anonymity."

"But you just told me your name."

"Yeah, well, I'm not recording at the moment."

"Okay... detective?"

"Call me Zack."

I blink. "Okay, Zack. I'm not sure what you want from me here. I only saw most of those guys a few times. I have no idea where they went."

"Right. Well, see, the thing is... I'm not sure I believe you." He chuckles again, but the laughter dies pretty quickly at my affronted expression. "Ah, sorry. Um, I'm looking into them. These men all have some common factors."

"They all dated me," I say through gritted teeth.

"Yeah, and most of them were... kinda messed up dudes."

"I didn't know any of that when I met them."

He nods, but it feels placating. "Listen, I'm going about this wrong. I came here to see if you'd be up for an interview. I'm trying to do a new piece for the podcast. Cops aren't getting anywhere with these missing people. These ones," he gestures to a few names on the list, "have been given up on entirely. No bodies, no tracks, nothing. It's a mystery."

His eyes light up as he turns back to me.

A smidgen of a smile jerks at my lips. "A mystery?"

"Yeah." He grins like a kid in a candy store.

"You had a detective kit growing up, didn't you?" I ask.

He laughs again, the sound thick and infectious. A chuckle bubbles up from me before I can stop it.

"So, would you be up for an interview?"

I glance at the clock. "I have plans tonight, and I was supposed to lock up a couple minutes ago. Maybe this weekend?"

He nods eagerly.

We exchange numbers, and I hop onto the socials to follow his podcast account. It's bigger than I expected.

I walk him to the door to lock it behind him when a thought occurs to me. "Hey."

He looks back, those eyes still alight with excitement.

"Am I like... a suspect for you?"

"Uh." He swallows, and I immediately realize the answer is a resounding yes.

I gape at him for a moment, waiting.

"Well, let's see how the interview goes, yeah? Everyone's a suspect until they give an alibi, right?"

"I'm pretty sure everyone is innocent until proven guilty."

"Suspect doesn't mean guilty."

I huff a grudging chuckle and nod. "All alright, but just so you know, I've been cleared by the cops already."

He laughs and even with the heat of mild frustration and a bit of embarrassment, I can't help smiling at the sound.

"See you this weekend," he says, and strides away down the street.

I flip the deadbolt and lean on the glass. "Fuck."

"Two guys in one day?"

I don't respond. Talking and mascara don't go well together.

"I'm not judging," Zoe adds. "But if tonight goes well, are you just gonna cancel on the weekend dude?"

I stick the wand back in the tube and adjust my lashes so there aren't any little black clumps. "The weekend dude isn't a date. He's a true crime podcaster."

Zoe cocks her head to the side. "What does he want with you?"

I roll my eyes. "Well, turns out more men from my past are missing than I thought. Though, given what we know about men from my past, they could be hiding from the mob or something."

She nods. "Or in witness protection."

I huff a sigh, digging through my collection of lipstick for the perfect blood red color. "Given my—" *finger quotes*—"'track record,' I doubt any of them have done something as decent as testify against someone bad enough to get witness protection."

Zoe chuckles and leans into my side with an arm around my shoulder. "They weren't all that bad."

I grumble something like, "Motherfuckers," under my breath.

"Indeed. Well, good luck tonight. I'll be in my room by the time you get back…"

The unasked question hangs in the air.

"Possibly not alone," I answer. "I'll text you if I'm bringing him back for a movie or something."

"A movie. Riiiiight." She gives me a mischievous grin. I lightheartedly shove her from my bedroom and put the final touches on my immaculate make-up.

Damn, I'm good.

Trent is early. Take that, track record. He has seats for us at the bar and, as I'd predicted, the man cleans up good. His hair is washed, with that damp look that might be attributed to a recent shower or gel. He's rocking a three-quarter fold on the sleeves of his button-up and the tightness of his jeans suggests he doesn't skip leg day.

He lets out a breath as I step forward, his gaze scanning me from head to toe as I watch with a cocky smile.

"Like what you see?" I ask with a twirl, chuckling as he nods appreciatively.

"Definitely."

"Your turn."

His mouth opens a little as confusion clouds his face. I laugh.

"Spin, Trent. Let's see the goods."

He laughs too, takes a step away from the bar, and does a half-decent twirl.

"Very nice," I say with a grin.

We settle on the stools, he waves the bartender over, and the food and drink begin to flow.

We exchange the usual first date banter. He's got three brothers and a handful of cousins. I've got Zoe. He moved here a couple years ago for college. I never graduated, and moved here barely a month ago. We find common ground in movies and TV shows. Neither of us goes for crime docs or thrillers; we like funny action. He doesn't have any pets but has always wanted a dog.

It's a nice date. Nicer than Derek by a longshot, but I had given him the benefit of the doubt. As Zoe keeps saying, I've got to stop doing that.

We head back to my and Zoe's place for a movie and some microwave popcorn. Knight and Day should be a laugh. We both think Tom Cruise is a weirdo but love his movies.

"Oh," I say in a low voice as we step across the thresh-old, "we don't need to be crazy quiet or anything, but my roommate is home so I don't want to be over-the-top loud."

He nods and gives a thumbs up.

"Also if you could take off your shoes." I gesture to the shoe rack Zoe spent a good three hours measuring, cutting, sanding, and painting. It's dang cute and, like everything she does, matches the rest of the apartment perfectly.

Above it hangs a bracelet I made in the 4th grade. It's Zoe's—my first present to her. It's become something of a good luck charm at this point, we each touch it before leaving the house. The dang thing is fraying, the little pink elephants starting to fade to an off-white color, but neither of us can throw it away.

This time, Trent gives an eyeroll. I flash a smile as I undo the laces on my boots. I've rolled my eyes about a hundred times over the no-shoe rule myself.

Trent settles onto the long, L-shaped couch that barely fits in the living room. He lightly touches a few of the leaves from the dangling spider plant on the side table. "Sure is clean in here."

"Yeah, Zoe is a bit of a clean-freak. Makes my life easier though."

He shrugs.

I put on the movie and hurry into the kitchen to get the popcorn going. I dump the goods into a big wooden bowl and snuggle in beside Trent. He lifts his arm. His sturdy frame isn't quite as comfy as the plush pillows Zoe and I found at a thrift store near our place, but the feel of his muscles sends a rush of heat to my stomach.

We hit the halfway point in the movie when the popcorn runs out.

"Got any more snacks?" he asks with a grin.

"Ha. Dessert later, if you're lucky."

There's a second of blank on his face before it clicks, and he laughs.

"Let me go see if I can dig out some ice cream." I leave the movie on and go find a pint of mint chip in the freezer. I shovel a few scoops into two mugs and bring them out.

On my way back in to put the ice cream away, Trent comes up behind me with a hug around my waist.

"Hey, handsome," I say with a grin.

"Come back to the movie. I'm getting lonely in there."

I chuckle. "I'll be in in a sec. I've gotta put this away and wipe down the counter."

He laughs. "Wipe the counter? Why?"

I toss him a glance as I wet the sponge. "Ice cream? Sticky?"

He shrugs and puts on a pouty face as though this is going to take more than twenty seconds. "Seems like you could just do it in the morning." He turns around and mopes back to the couch.

"Okaaayyyy," I mutter to myself.

I wipe where the pint had sat, dry it down, and hang the towel. When I return to the living room, Trent has already finished his mug.

"We might need to go somewhere that serves bigger courses next time," I say with a laugh. "Thanks for waiting." I gesture to the TV where the movie is paused.

"Yeah." He reaches out, and I sink half onto the couch and half onto his lap. "Didn't want you to miss it to clean a stupid counter."

I let out a lightly forced laugh. "My friend has a way she likes things. I don't mind."

"Whatever." He stretches, putting his arm around me and caressing my shoulder. "She sounds like a bitch."

My ears ring. Ice seems to form in my veins as every ounce of heat I had for this man evaporates.

"Hey, I have an idea," I say, standing and giving him a flirty look.

He meets it with a shifting lust-filled grin.

My look slides into a sneer. "Get the fuck out of my apartment."

"What?" The lusty glow goes out like a light.

"You heard me. You seemed like a nice guy, but no nice guy calls someone he's never met a 'bitch'. And no one... *no one*, calls my best friend that."

"You for real?" He stands, and I take a step back, my brow still in a furrowed glare.

"Yep. Leave. Now. And lose my number on your way out."

"Fucking missing out, bitch."

"There's that super fun word again." I toss him a sarcastic smile. My phone is in my hand now, fingers clicking the screen as I dial 911. I hover over the little green call icon—just in case.

"Fine. You're probably a sloppy fuck anyway."

Heat roils through my chest. I clench my jaw and inhale through my nose like Dr. Suzie – my old therapist – taught me. Breathe. Count to ten. If you still feel like slapping someone after that, maybe they deserve it.

Okay, that last part was Zoe after I told her about our sessions, but it seems like good advice to me.

By the time I reach 8, he's at the door. No slapping today.

He jerks the door open, flips me off, and slams it shut behind him. I wait exactly four seconds before darting over and throwing both the deadbolt and linking up the chain.

I trudge to the kitchen, scoop another dollop of mint chip into my mug, and heave a sigh. To no one in particular, or maybe to the ice cream, I say, "Pity. He was really hot."

CHAPTER FOUR

TRUE CRIME TOM

"He's lucky I didn't hear him call you a bitch," I growl.

Karrie lifts a shoulder as she scrubs the remnants of her scrambled eggs out of the pan. "He called you one, too."

"That's not really a surprise. I *am* a bitch." I lean against the wall and fold my arms. "You, however, are not." It's clear she doesn't actually sense how much I'm seething. Which is probably a good thing. Murderous is not an exaggeration right now.

"Well, like you always say, I don't have the greatest taste in men." She sounds so defeated for a minute that I hate myself for making her feel bad about it, even if it is absolutely true.

I hold myself very still as she sets the clean pan into the drying rack and rolls her head, popping her neck. I can see her shifting gears and sliding back into light and bubbly Karrie. She shoots me her brilliant smile so suddenly that I wince because it's nearly blinding. And the most galling part of it is that she genuinely has shed the irritation of the disaster of a date from the night before. Which tells me it's not that big of a deal, and this guy will get to breathe another day.

Fortunately for my lucky sweater.

"Forget about him." She waves her hands in the air as if she's literally erasing him from existence. "I scheduled a late lunch with the other guy."

I laugh darkly, shaking my head. "Of course you did." I raise a brow. "I thought it wasn't supposed to be a date."

Her eyes shift away from my face. "It isn't. It's just an interview."

"Karrie," I say in warning.

"What? He's cute!"

I snort, rolling my eyes as I push away from the wall and follow her out to the living room. "That explains the pants."

She stops short, hands landing on her thighs as she looks down at herself. "What's wrong with my pants?"

"They're your ass pants," I say flatly, dubious that she is that clueless. If anyone knows they're hot, it's Karrie. She uses it to her advantage on a regular basis.

She laughs. "My ass pants?"

Or maybe she isn't aware—at least of the pants. "Yeah, hands-down the most flattering to your ass. I guess you wouldn't know since you can't see it like the rest of us can."

She pirouettes, spinning so suddenly to hug me, I'm not prepared at first. "You give me the best ego boosts. And that is why you are the best best friend."

I hug her back. "Damn right I am. Which is why I'm coming to this late lunch."

She pulls back and gives me the most exaggerated gasp I have to laugh. "Zoe Turner is going out in public?! Without being bribed, threatened, or inebriated?" Her eyes narrow. "Wait, *are* you high?"

I give her a dark look as she cackles and spins back around, heading for her bedroom. And if I know Karrie, it's so she can primp and preen. She might be about to walk into an interview about possibly being connected to the disappearances of several men she's dated, but it's a meeting with an allegedly attractive man. And Karrie never passes up the opportunity to make a guy fall all over himself for her.

Because one, she's damn good at it. And two, she enjoys it so much. I'd never dream of talking her out of it. Even if it seems ill-advised.

I lean against her doorway as she plops down at her vanity, confirming my suspicions as she flutters her fingers over her varied supply of beauty products. She picks up her brush first.

"So, why are you coming with me to this interview?" she asks, brushing through her thick hair, which she's left down—by far, the best way to style it for her face.

"Aforementioned terrible taste in men notwithstanding?" I ask, raising a brow.

The reflection in her vanity mirror gives me a great view of her sticking her tongue out at me before she proceeds with applying her usual thick eyeliner. She's lucky she has such large eyes. On anyone else, it would be gaudy. It just makes her look more exotic.

"Honestly, I don't need to sit in on the interview. Or meet him. I want to be there just in case. Sit in the background."

"Like a stake-out?" she asks, her eyes lighting up. "Stake him out while he's staking me out. Me likey. Just like old times." She holds up two lipsticks, pursing her lips in thought as she weighs her options.

"The darker one," I suggest. "Maybe if I did this more often, we could avoid the whole shitty dates and disappearing douchebags thing."

"That would require coming to clubs with me every weekend." She claps her hands with glee and spins to look at me. "I love this idea!"

I stick my finger in my mouth and fake-gag. "Maybe we could start with not meeting guys at clubs. How about a coffee shop?"

She pouts. "Okay, first of all, I met Trent from last night at a smoothie shop. Is that not classy enough for you? And second of all, it doesn't actually matter where I meet them. You hate all people anyway."

I sniff, feigning offense as she spreads the richer red lipstick over her lips.

We both know she is absolutely right, though hate is a strong word. There aren't many people I hate, but there aren't many I like either. Frankly, I rarely find people I think are worthy of my time, so I don't waste it.

"Make that a habit, and we'll see," I say. "It's much easier to focus on reading in a coffee shop than a club."

She pops her lips at herself and rolls her eyes. "What is the point of going if you're just planning to read the whole time?"

"To enjoy myself?" I shoot back. "And keep an eye on you." She opens her mouth to argue, but I plow ahead. "*Anyway*, I've already checked out True Crime Tom's podcast—"

Her brow wrinkles, and she spins to face me again. "His name is Zack, and his podcast is called—"

"Armchair Detective. Yes, I know." It's like she doesn't even know I'm a cyber stalker to the max. Oh, wait.

"Why do you always do this?"

I give her a blank stare.

"The nickname thing?" she prompts.

I continue to stare.

"And why Tom? It's so random."

"Alliteration." Seriously, how long has she known me?

She waits for further explanation, which I don't give. Because it should be obvious why I picked it, aside from the alliteration thing. That nickname is genius. Frankly, they all are. It gives me some way to identify the revolving door of dudes she's had in her life. And she only knows of the ones who are still alive. If only she knew what nicknames I'd given her missing dates. Trashbag Douchebag was only the most recent. I got a good chuckle out of that one.

She throws her hands into the air when the silence stretches. "You're impossible."

I shrug, but I can see the amused smirk on my face in her mirror as she goes to her closet to debate about her outfit, probably for the third, and definitely not the last, time.

I flip through my clever nicknames again to amuse myself. She needs very little encouragement because she knows what accentuates her assets and how to give off the right vibe.

There was Handsy Harry. I don't recall his real name, but he was the one who'd been convicted of sexual assault as a teen. Yeah, that record was supposed to be sealed, but I'm a keyboard wizard. Which also led me to the fact that he didn't leave his past in the past. Unfortunately for him, he hadn't been a hit it and quit it kinda guy. His plans for Karrie were varied and sadistic. Mine for him had been quick and lethal.

Karrie changes her top, analyzing herself in her full-length mirror. We both know she's sticking with her ass pants.

I nod my approval when she turns to me in her black—big surprise—v-neck tank top that's cut just low enough to show a little, but not so much that she seems like she's trying too hard. I know she's going to wear her cropped leather jacket on top, and she'll probably add her leopard print ankle boots to the outfit.

There was Reject Richard, the guy who had a serious issue anytime a woman turned him down. Karrie had started talking about breaking up with him when I found the list of previous assaults and two missing women who'd rejected him in the past. I wasn't the first to dump him, but I was definitely the first to dump him in a river.

I snap myself out of my reverie and follow her back out to the living room. "You know what would go nicely with those black jeans and your black leather jacket and your black earrings?"

She curls her lip, already knowing what I'm going to suggest. "Don't say your hot pink silk tank, Zoe. It's not going to happen."

"But you'd look so good in it!"

She pats my cheek. "You look better in it."

"True."

True Crime Tom is no slouch, that's for damn sure. Alleged has turned to confirmed. He probably works out regularly. A runner, maybe. Nothing crazy. He's not the type. Not obsessive, nor overly into himself or his looks.

And the more I observe him—the easy way he moves and his lithe frame—I realize he probably runs for the hell of it. He fucking likes it. I can just tell he's one of those.

Running just clears my head. When I hit my stride, I get that rush.

Blech. I hate running.

I'm sitting close enough to hear them, so I don't have to stare at them like a weirdo as they talk, though I glance over at regular but totally normal intervals.

She's being Karrie. Warm and friendly, always a little flirty. She can't help it.

TCT is a gentleman, though he's clearly enjoying the chat. Maybe flirting a little back. But in the nice guy way. He hasn't even tried to look down her shirt.

I narrow my eyes in suspicion. Maybe he's gay.

"So, Karrie," TCT says. "You said you weren't aware six of the men you've dated have gone missing, all not long after you dated them."

I stiffen, my fingers around the coffee shop's mug going white. Six?

"Um, no, actually. I knew of, like, three," she replies. There's the slightest tremble in her voice.

I glance up in time to see her tuck some loose hair behind her ear.

"Derek Waters was the most recent." He sets a picture on the table between them.

I see the file he has in his lap that he's going to pull more pictures from. Look at TCT being all detective-y. Very theatrical. He's even watching her face super closely as he lays another photo in front of her. Like he's been trained to do this.

"Before that, it was Adam Delaney."

Right. Adam Delaney was *Handsy Harry*.

Another photo. "Jeremy Hicks."

Reject Richard.

"Marcus Kennedy."

I flinch. Marcus Kennedy. I actually really liked that guy. Okay, not liked. Tolerated. He had been a decent pick of Karrie's. He'd laughed too much and too loudly, but that wasn't a punishable offense. And I definitely hadn't had a hand in his disappearance.

"Jackson Rojas."

Uh huh. *Puppy Puncher*. He'd had some seriously deep-seeded issues to be that cruel to animals. A serial killer waiting to happen.

I'd know.

"David Van Zuiden."

Didn't even know who that guy was. I chanced a look at Karrie, whose shocked face gives me a slight pang of guilt.

"And Vincent Marone."

Oh, yeah. *Vincent*. No nickname for him because he was my first. He was the one who'd started this whole thing.

I watch Karrie's face carefully. Her shocked expression morphed a little at his picture. Her gaping mouth closes so she can clench her jaw against a reaction. The emotions—for both of us—are raw, even a decade later.

Vincent had been a doozy. Particularly because he was my first, but also because he'd actually hurt her before I got to him. He's the reason I never let these other assholes get that far with Karrie. Take them out before it can happen again. And, if it isn't Karrie, it would be someone else falling victim.

"You recognize them all," TCT says, his eyes very intent on Karrie's face.

Duh. Of course she recognizes them. She dated them all. Unfortunately.

Even though T.C.T is basically playacting at being a detective, the hardness that comes with being a seasoned police officer doesn't affect him, so he isn't too rough around the edges. In fact, he's being pretty gentle with her.

So, True Crime Tom gets to stay out of the murder book that exists only in my mind—because I'm not a freaking idiot— for the moment. But I haven't done any research on him yet, so the jury's still out on how long that will be the case.

"The thing is," Tom continues when she remains silent, "after looking into all of these men, each one of them has quite a sullied, and oftentimes violent, past."

I fight back my instinct to high-five myself for getting rid of these guys, not only for Karrie's benefit, but for the world at large. Who knew what they might have done if I'd let them live? But I maintain my composure, flipping a page in my book to keep up my ruse.

Karrie, though, takes in the information with confusion and a little bit of dismay, which is only noticeable to me because I know her so well. That little line forms between her brows, and her fingers stiffen in her lap.

True Crime Tom's gaze narrows a little, though he doesn't go all steely like I expect. Maybe he's not an idiot and can see this is all news to her. When he starts diving into boring questions, like *What draws you to these men?* and *How serious was each relationship?* I decide the jury's still out on the idiot part.

I take the opportunity to go to the bathroom just so I don't have to listen to it. Maybe when I get back, he'll be getting into the nitty-gritty and have something to give me. Or maybe he'll be half in love with Karrie and lose track of his goal with the interview, which I'm still not a fan of anyway.

But if that's the case, I would rather head home to nose into his past and see what kind of guy he really is—true crime Columbo or a lame-o who just regurgitates what he reads in the papers.

When I leave the restroom, I spy TCT up at the counter ordering something. Looks like a water in a to-go cup. Karrie is sitting alone at the table, twisted in her seat so that she can shoot me a very significant look.

I mouth *what?* though I know damn well what she's trying to communicate because, one, I'm an excellent non-verbal communicator, and two, because I know Karrie better than anyone. Probably better than she knows herself.

She gives me a glare and jerks her thumb discreetly to the door.

I release a sigh as I stalk past her to collect my stuff from my table, making sure she hears how drawn-out and dramatic it is.

I turn and push the door with my back and raise an eyebrow at Karrie as I go just as TCT rejoins her at their table.

Chapter Five

ACCUSED

Zoe's bemused expression sits in my brain for a while as Zack and I leave the coffee shop and head down to the river. There's a beautiful trail with a nice amount of shade and enough foot traffic that I don't mind walking alone with a guy I don't know very well.

That being said, I wouldn't mind getting to know him better...

"You didn't know he was dead?"

The question pulls me from my hopes of turning the conversation towards a more date-like atmosphere.

"Vincent?" Stupid question, who else would it be? "I had no idea. I knew he dipped town after we broke up." My hands twist together, fingers nearly going white with the effort of keeping my voice steady. "It wasn't exactly a mutual thing."

"Rough breakup?"

I watch the ground as we walk. Rough breakup—what a way to put it. "Do you mind if we stop recording for a minute?"

Zack's eyes widen a bit, but he nods. He flicks a switch on his little mic and unplugs it from his phone. We cross to a bench and sit.

He doesn't speak, waiting for me to fill the silence. I continue to fidget.

"We don't have to talk about it."

I shake my head. "It's fine. Just embarrassing."

He raises an eyebrow.

I heave a sigh. "I've dated a lot of idiots and assholes."

He nods with an expression so much like Zoe that I give an eye roll.

"He's the only guy I've dated who turned *me* into an idiot and an asshole."

Zack lets out a little huff of a laugh. "I doubt that."

"I was seventeen when we started dating. He was twenty-six. It was dumb, and I was dumb."

"What happened?"

Tension squeezes my stomach, and I grimace. "I moved in with him as soon as I turned eighteen. I was still in high school. My parents didn't care but my bestie, Zoe, hated it. I was infatuated and, again, dumb."

I lean forward, resting my forearms on my knees.

"He wasn't a good guy. It took me way too long to realize it. When it finally clicked, I dumped him and moved back home." I swallow, trying to decide how much to tell

Zack. He already kind of suspects me of murder. Telling him about all the shit Vincent put me through isn't going to paint me as innocent. "Eventually he left town."

That's about the truth of it. Vincent was a walking gaslight machine. The guy convinced me he was the only person I could trust. He isolated me from everyone in my life, so when the hitting started, it felt like I had no one to turn to.

No one but Zoe.

Because no matter what I said to her, how often I canceled plans or made excuses, she was always there. Once a week, like clockwork, she'd show up at the door, push past Vincent if he was home, and insist on a girl's movie night. It was that presence that let me know there was somewhere to run to when the time came.

I shake my head and pinch my lips between my teeth. "I, uh, sorry. I don't like talking about him." My throat is tight; I swallow. "When did he die?"

Zack leans forward as well, turning his head to meet my eye. "The police don't know. His body was found a few years ago. Well, what was left of it."

I grimace and sit straight. "Gross."

I lean back a bit and Zack straightens as well, still studying me.

"His murder is still a mystery," Zack says.

I look away from his piercing gaze and take in our view of the lake. Sunlight glints across the surface, making me wish I'd brought my chunky cheetah-print sunglasses. I inhale, breathing in the fresh air around us. Zoe and I moved just before the leaves started changing color. They litter the ground now, only hints of red and gold still on the trees.

I let out my breath with a sigh.

"Impressive detective work." I try to smile. "I'm surprised you connected us. The cops didn't ask me about him."

"Cops?"

I heave a sigh; we'd stuck to missing men at the coffee shop. I didn't tell him about the round of questioning I already went through yesterday.

"They brought me in about Derek because I was one of the last people to see him."

Zack's eyes narrow. "The police said that?"

"Yeah, why?"

He purses his lips. "Nothing just..." He runs a hand through his dark hair. The bend of his arm highlights the muscles I knew were hiding under his shirt.

My breath catches despite the seriousness of the conversation. I glance at the buttons on his shirt. I wonder how much chiseling we are working with here. And how *can* I get this conversation in a more date-like line of questioning?

"Karrie?"

"Huh? Oh, sorry. What did you say?"

He tilts his head, looking slightly perplexed. "I said um... Did you kill them?"

Time and sound stop for a few seconds as I process the question. I'm starting to think a date isn't a possibility.

"No." I turn to face him, glancing at the mic. It's still off, though I'm sure this is plenty of juicy stuff for the podcast. "I didn't kill them. I don't kill the guys I date. They just…"

Unease and uncertainty stir in my stomach.

"Look," I slash the air with my hand and Zack jerks back; I roll my eyes. "With the guys I date, they either like me and I think they're lame, or I like them and they completely ghost me."

His eyes go wide.

"Knock it off," I snap. "I'm talking about our current social use of the term, not literal ghosts. Jeez."

He laughs.

Not the reaction I was expecting, but I can't help a soft chuckle as he clutches his gut. "I figured. I was just wondering what a guy has to do to be considered lame."

"Oh." I shake my head. "I had a date last night, and he just ended up being a dick. I kicked him out before the movie ended."

Zack glances at the folder sitting under the mic and his phone. It's thick, stuffed with police reports, press releases, and crime scene pictures I said I had no interest in looking at. Bodies aren't really my thing. At least, not dead ones.

"Maybe that's a good thing for him…"

A chill runs down my spine. I lick my lips, the faint lingering cherry taste of my lipstick mixing with the coffee still on my tongue. "Right. I, uh, I didn't think of that."

We sit in slightly uncomfortable silence for a while. My thoughts whirl. Vincent is dead. More than a handful of guys I've dated have gone missing. I wonder briefly about the women I've dallied with, but that feels unlikely. I'm still friends with most of them. What about the ones before Vincent? The half a dozen dates I went on in high school, to a movie, an arcade, dumb fun stuff that ended with a kiss and me letting them know I wasn't looking for something serious?

Zoe was always ready with a good excuse to get me out of a second date.

My gaze is still fixed on the folder. What does this mean for me now? Is every guy I date going to disappear? How many of them are still alive?

The scone and coffee in my stomach suddenly feel out of place. I swallow down that metallic spit that comes before throwing up.

"I think I'm going to go," I mutter.

Zack stands with me, worry pinching his forehead and lips. "Is everything—"

"Okay? Not really. I just found out that dating me might be a one-way ticket to the missing persons department."

"Right." He sighs. "Listen, I didn't mean to just dump this on you. I wanted to find out–"

"If I'm a murderer?" I interrupt again.

He nods as though there's nothing odd or wrong with him thinking that.

I shake my head. "This is making me sick. I didn't do anything to those men. I didn't..." I pause to breathe through a fresh wave of nausea. "I don't know *what* happened to them."

"Do you want to find out?"

Once again Zack has said just the right thing to freeze my instincts.

"What?"

"Well, I'm following this story," he says with a shrug, gesturing to his stuff on the bench. "I want to find out what happened. This will make for a really good series."

"Armchair Detective."

"Exactly."

"Do your listeners know you aren't actually sitting in an armchair?"

He cracks a grin. "I get it if this isn't your thing, but you are still kind of a suspect. If you want to help clear your name, and find the truth, I could always use a Nancy Drew to my Hardy Boy routine."

A smile breaks through the nerves. "What if someone thinks we're dating? You might be the next to go missing."

His expression darkens. "That's a risk I'm willing to take to find out the truth."

I bite my lip. "Yeah, okay. It wouldn't be the worst thing to know how Vincent died and to make sure the cops can't pin any of this on me if they decide to come back around."

"Smoothie in a couple days?" He scoops up his supplies, and we start a slow stroll back toward the coffee shop.

I make a face. "Something less date-like. Library?"

He shrugs. "Sure. I can get you up to speed on the particulars of the disappearances." He spins, walking backward and looking me directly in the eye. "Unless you already know and you're just a really good liar…"

This time, I laugh. Part of him is probably serious, but the joke of me being a murder suspect is pretty funny.

"I guess you'll find out."

He smirks, skipping back into stride with me. "I guess I will."

Zoe is as sprawled as she gets on the living room couch when I get home. She'd sit like a robot if it didn't start an ache in her long legs. Instead she props a pillow behind her back, extends her legs rod-straight along the couch, and has a perfect view of both the television and door.

She doesn't even glance away from the TV. "How'd the rest of your date go?"

"Wasn't a date," I say as I remove my shoes, tuck them on the shelf, and hang my purse on the coat hook.

"Sounded like it was going to become one when I left."

I move into the kitchen, in need of tea and a notepad to make a shopping list. "Yeah, well it went from almost-date to accused of murder pretty quick."

The TV switches off. I glance over. Zoe is standing, eyes wide as she watches me.

"He still suspects you?"

I shrug. "I think it's partially a joke now? But, uh…" My jaw tightens. Even now, so many years later, bringing up Vincent slams a wave of guilt through me. "You'll never guess what happened to Vincent."

"He's dead."

I nearly drop my tea. "What? How did you know?"

Zoe rolls her eyes as she joins me in the kitchen, pouring herself a drink as well. "I heard the list of guys who are missing. So when you told me to kick rocks, I came home and did some research."

"Do you…" I gulp. "Do you know when he died?"

She shakes her head, a casual and uncaring expression on her face. "It was years after you broke up. The cops don't even know. Too much decomposition on the body."

"Hrmph."

That's it. The final words needed to make me expel my breakfast. I push past Zoe and into the bathroom, regurgitating everything within me as though the toilet is a baby bird in need of caffeine and pastries.

"Should I document this?" Zoe asks from the bathroom door. "As evidence that your stomach isn't strong enough for you to be a murderer?"

I flip her off, and she laughs.

A few minutes later, when I emerge from the bathroom, lightheaded but with freshly brushed teeth, she is waiting with a glass of ice water.

"You okay?"

I take the water, sip a bit, and shake my head. "I don't know, Zoe. It feels... completely surreal. I don't know what's going on, and that scares me."

"Can't feel good to have your exes brought up either."

I shake my head again.

"What can I do?"

A soft smile crosses my lips as she runs a hand up and down my arm. I lean my head on her shoulder and focus on breathing for a moment.

"Just be here with some ice water when I get back from scooby doo-ing with Zack on Saturday."

She stiffens. "You're doing what?"

I nod and pull away, hoisting myself onto the counter despite her grimace and sipping my water as I explain the plan.

"So..." Zoe heaves a sigh, pressing a hand to her forehead as exasperation wrinkles her nose. "You're going to go all detective with True Crime Tom?"

"Who?"

"You literally just went on a date with him." Her dry tone shows zero understanding that his name is *not* Tom.

"His name is Zack."

Her expression doesn't change. "Anyway, you're doing what exactly?"

"Well..." I fidget with the hem of my shirt. "I want—no. I *need* to know what happened to these guys, Zoe. What if I'm a curse?"

She rolls her eyes. "Ridiculous."

"Okay, well you can call me ridiculous after you've been responsible for half a dozen disappearances."

A weird look flashes across her face, then she shrugs. "Fine. But I'm detectiving with you."

I clap my hands together. "That's actually perfect. I was worried someone might think Zack and I are dating, but if you're there too—"

"No one will think you and True Crime Tom are doing the nasty," she finishes in a flat tone. "Perfect."

I laugh at the pained expression on her face. Then I hop off the counter and take a Clorox wipe to it real quick. "I'm starving. Sushi?"

Zoe squints at me, her mouth a little open, the hint of disgust on her face. "You're impossible, you know that?"

I wink. "Yep."

Chapter Six

SCOOBY DOO TOO

You'd think scooby-dooing would be my jam. After all, I'm a one-woman investigative powerhouse when it comes to digging into any subject. But my way is far superior because I don't have to go anywhere or interact with anyone.

If I didn't love Karrie so much—and honestly, she's the easiest person to live with anyway—I would absolutely live alone. Probably buy some land up in a remote area of the mountains. Maybe even in a cave if it had good wifi connection and a comfy couch.

A dark, quiet cave sounded good after I'd gotten up at the butt-crack of dawn to follow True Crime Tom on his—surprise!—morning run.

Because I often do my shopping and what errands I can before or after the average American, Karrie hadn't even stirred when I left this morning and didn't bat an eye when I returned home. After doing my due diligence in my internet search on one Zack Lim, host of the popular Armchair Detective podcast, I figured I'd do some real-time surveillance.

Creeping along in my car to watch him was pretty easy. He wasn't overly aware of his surroundings, though there was enough traffic for me to blend in decently. His route was somewhat predictable, mostly because it was the most logical (and popular) path.

My assumption about him liking to run was an understatement. Dude ran several miles with the easy lope of a seasoned athlete, and I spotted a grin on his face more than once during that time. Plus, he waved to several other avid runners on his route, which told me it was a frequent enough occurrence that he'd made friends.

So I'm already deeply entrenched in my suspicion of the man by the time we walk up to the front of the library where he waits for us.

"Zack, this is my best friend, Zoe," Karrie says with a grin.

He's got a laptop bag slung across his body, one hand gripping the strap across his chest. Despite the palpable awkwardness that hangs suspended between everyone because, you know, he thinks Karrie might be a murderer, he gives me a pretty winning smile. All straight, white teeth and dimples. He offers his hand.

I look down at it, debating about his level of conscientiousness and how likely it was he'd recently washed his hands. But the cleanliness of most men has always been particularly suspect to me, and I'm not willing to chance it.

I wrinkle my nose. "Nice to meet you. Sorry, I'm not much of a hand-shaker."

His thick brows wrinkle over his dark eyes, but he shrugs it off with surprising ease and leads the way into the library.

"Can you at least try to be nice?" Karrie says under her breath as she moves past me, flicking her dark braid over her shoulder.

I frown. "I was being nice."

She gives me a dark look as we follow TCT through the main area of the library to the tables toward the back.

I raise a brow. "Pretty sure preventing the spread of germs counts as being nice, but whatever."

Admittedly, I may be taking my borderline-OCD tendencies a little too far. But aside from socializing in general being the bane of my existence, I also hate going out in public because of the cleanliness—or lack thereof—that is obvious in every corner of society.

To placate her—since she is apparently still hoping some kind of relationship might develop out of this misadventure?—I plaster on a questionably non-psychotic smile. I can tell by the look on her face that it isn't very convincing, but she doesn't say anything as we keep moving through the stacks.

I've always loved the idea of libraries, but the realization that hundreds of hands might have touched the same books I am touching gives me the heebies.

My germaphobia and fastidiousness is honestly probably the main reason I've never gotten caught "taking care of" Karrie's backlog of douchebag dates. When you pay that much attention to those things, it's harder to leave evidence behind.

But, after doing research on True Crime Tom, I've come to have a healthy respect for his methods. Not only has he legitimately solved more than one cold case, his podcast is genuinely interesting to listen to, though I would never say that out loud to anyone.

So I'm grateful that I volunteered to join in the festivities and see his process firsthand. I've never put much stock in the police's ability to sniff me out, but they don't have the connecting thread—Karrie—that Tom has grasped onto. A thread that already puts this in the danger zone.

Because it's not like I can take Tom out of the picture if he gets too close to the truth. *That* would definitely be suspicious for anyone investigating since he's already onto Karrie's connection. And because most people aren't as antisocial as me, it's doubtful that he hasn't shared at least some of his theories with another person.

And if he suspects Karrie of being the murderer, he wouldn't be spending time with her without some kind of safety net in place. Unless he's an over-confident prick.

Which isn't out of the realm of possibility. Still working on gauging that part.

So my only option is to subtly lead this investigation down the wrong path and keep myself—and Karrie—off the list of suspects.

My work may be cut out for me. The laptop he pulls out of his bag is fancy as shit, and he's got a manila folder stuffed to bursting with papers. And they're labeled. Meticulously.

He plops the folder onto the table and opens his laptop, getting ready to sit. Karrie pulls a chair up next to him, overtly flouncing with enthusiasm, which elicits an eye roll from me.

I opt to stand, folding my arms across my middle, and clutch my elbows. Anything to keep from touching anything. My eyes bounce around the room.

A mother of three is carrying a stack of picture books and her three year old has just smeared an unidentified food-like substance on the table closest to us. And that college kid on the other side of us is sniffling rather violently.

Definitely not going to sit.

"Zoe, would you like to sit?" TCT asks as if reading my mind.

I almost scoff at his polite tone, but then I realize it's one hundred percent genuine. "I'm good, thanks."

"Okay. Well, I promise I don't bite." He offers me a wink.

"I'm good," I answer, though it's not what I actually want to say, which is that I can't promise the same thing.

But my answer is satisfying enough because he turns to pull up whatever files he wants to show us, I guess.

"Just wanted you guys to see that what I have for this new segment is getting a lot of traction on the podcast."

"What segment?" I ask flatly. Is this just to prove how cool he is and how great his podcast is doing? Then why the hell am I here? That shit only works on Karrie.

Which is very clear as she sits forward, looking incredibly intrigued. And I can't honestly tell if she's genuinely interested or just giving him the ego boost.

"I started this black widow style investigative episode where I talk about cases like Karrie's."

I narrow my eyes at him, not liking the implication.

"People find this sort of thing fascinating. Women who snapped."

Now Karrie mirrors my expression as she pulls back to look at him.

"Karrie isn't a black widow." My grip on my elbows becomes painful. "*She* didn't kill anyone." *Nope. That would be me.*

True Crime Tom looks up at me, his expression morphing, like he'd forgotten who he was even with. Then he glances at Karrie, who's also staring at him, though probably not as murderously.

"I just—" he clears his throat loudly and shifts forward in his seat— "Not all of the women I mentioned are—or appear to be—guilty. It's just the overarching... um... theme." He scratches the back of his neck as Karrie and I continue to stare at him, and I relish his discomfort.

He expels a breath. "I think it will go pretty far to have you on, Karrie. As part of the investigation, but also at the end. When we prove that you aren't a killer."

He continues to stumble over his words, but he has a point about listeners being super into the idea of hearing from a woman at the center of this kind of controversy. It makes sense that his numbers are so high with this segment, considering he's the one who connected Karrie with all these missing men.

Even if he was mediocre, I'd be tempted to tune in just to see how it played out.

The sniffling college student falls into a coughing fit, and I squeeze myself tighter, shifting farther away from him. "Listen, are we going to do real investigating or just talk about your little radio show?"

TCT frowns, glancing at the coughing guy then back to me. "Um, podcast. But, yeah, we can get started." He clicks out of whatever program he was in and pulls up a document. "This is a timeline I've been working on."

I shift to stand behind them both to look at what he has. Very thorough. Has the necessary details (alleged last interaction with Karrie then date and time of being reported missing), clean and sharp and color-coded. It truly is a thing of beauty.

"What's this?" I point to a couple of off-shoots with names and question marks.

Karrie doesn't turn, but she reaches back and grabs my hand.

"I found a few interesting connections," TCT says, oblivious to Karrie's death grip and the subsequent loss of feeling in my fingers.

"Connections?" I ask, though I can clearly see two names on there I may or may not have been (definitely was) responsible for.

"Four more men that have come up in my research," TCT explains with a nod. "I haven't figured out if they're officially on the list."

"Why?" Karrie asks. Her voice is very small, and I'm happily hating TCT again.

"Well, the deaths of these two," he points, "are suspicious but haven't been ruled as foul play."

"So then why connect them to Karrie at all?" I ask, a very particularly sharp edge to my tone.

He looks at me, real regret in his eyes. "Because she interacted with them not long before they died."

I glare at him because, one, I hate the implication. Two, because we knew nothing about this. And three, because he found out this information, and I didn't.

"I had no idea they were dead," Karrie whispers, and I think surely this is the last straw, and we get to be done with scooby-dooing.

"How'd they die?" I demand, scooching another step sideways when College Cougher descends into a phlegmatic fit again.

"One drowned during a trip to the river. The other in a car crash. Faulty brakes." The skepticism in his voice on that last one definitely matches how I feel. Faulty brakes sounds suspicious as hell in any circumstance.

The drowning, not as much. But lined up next to the car fatality, its dubious cause, and Karrie's—ahem—history, it's clear there's a frightening pattern. Plus, I'm pretty sure the drowned guy was Surf Bro, whom she had a fling with a few years back. Not long after Vincent, if I recall.

Maybe I picked the wrong method of protecting my friend from deviants. Because I'm worried she genuinely might be cursed, and not just with a homicidal best friend.

"I can't..." Karrie has that choked *I'm-about-to-throw-up* look about her, so I figure it's a good time to end her misery.

"Hey, you know what, Tom, I think Karrie and I need to head home for some good, old-fashioned disassociating." I slip a hand around her arm and tug. "Ya know, wine, rom-coms, a gallon of ice cream. So, how about we call it a day?"

His eyes go wide and concerned as he takes in her pallid complexion. "Karrie, I'm so sorry! I didn't mean to upset you."

I hold up a hand. "Save it, Columbo. We just need a break."

Karrie says nothing as I practically drag her out of Library of Germs, and she sucks in a sharp breath as soon as the brisk autumn breeze whooshes into our faces.

"Oh my God," is all she says as I speed-walk us to the car and stuff her in.

"It's nothing, Karrie," I assure her as I climb in behind the wheel.

"I'm poison," she says. "Toxic. A black mark. They touch me, and they die."

My gut twists that my favorite person—no, literally the only person I like at all—would believe this about herself. "No," I growl.

"You're always telling me I have the worst taste in men. But I am just the worst."

"Nope, nope, nope. It's all a coincidence." And it's all my fault. Son of a bitch. "Bad luck is all. And it's the past."

She curls against the window. "Stop trying to make me feel better."

I've been friends with Karrie long enough to know when my words won't do anything. But it's also been long enough that I know when I need to bring out the big guns: ice cream, The Princess Bride, mani-pedi (I've been saving some leopard print nail wraps for a special occasion), and a hair braiding sesh. It probably sounds stupid and childish. But even I enjoy having someone play with my hair when I'm upset.

Two days later, Karrie breezes into the living room wearing the ass pants. I'm lounging on the couch, reading a book that honestly could have used another sweep by an editor.

"Tom—er, Zack," she shakes her head, "invited us over for some more scooby-dooing."

I curl my lip, imagining a bachelor pad cesspool. Mismatched garage sale couches with a sordid history of ass dents, three stacks of used dishes in various places throughout, a mound of laundry that's a mixture of both clean and dirty that he is unable to distinguish and so he takes outfits from both...

"Invited us over?" I shiver. "As in, to his place?"

"It's his studio, but yeah. He thought you might be more comfortable there than the library." She bounces her way into the kitchen.

Brownie points for Tom on that one, but still I squint at her as she goes through the process of making herself a sandwich. "I figured you wouldn't want to scooby any more."

She was dark and twisty over the result of the last session, though our girl pity party lifted her spirits a bit as we competed to see who could get the best timing as we quoted along with our movie. Plus, the leopard print nails were a huge hit. I went with bright pink, as usual.

She glances at me and quickly away. "I have to prove I'm innocent."

The ass pants say otherwise. I suspect it also has to do with the fact that Tom and Karrie seriously have a vibe going. Like a *I'm-into-you-but-the-whole-murder-thing-might-be-a-problem* vibe.

It's why I did another deep dive on his life and past. Pretty damn clean. Minus one little hiccup that honestly wouldn't be a red flag for me to do anything about. If I see things heating up between them, I might mention it to her. But it's definitely not kiddie-porn level by any means, so it can stay buried for the moment.

I sigh and theatrically set my mediocre best-seller (could've fooled me) on the side table. "When are we going?"

"As soon as I'm done eating," she answers with her mouth full.

We do our ritualistic tap of the bracelet on the wall as we leave.

The drive over to his studio is short. I find myself frowning the whole time. Karrie reminds me to try to be nice, so I stick out my tongue. But then I throw my arm around her and give her a squeeze as we walk up the steps because I recognize the nerves she tries to hide from the rest of the world.

Her voice is breathless as she grins and says "hi" when Tom opens the door. He actually seems a little nervous when he welcomes us in, running his hands through his dark hair as his eyes dart around the space.

It's actually impressively and meticulously tidy, and I spot the cleaning spray and the cloth on the edge of a table.

He actually blushes when he catches me looking at it. "I did a deep clean of the place for you, Zoe. I was just wiping down the last surfaces."

Karrie looks at me with a stupid grin and wide eyes, and I scrunch my face as Tom turns his back to us.

Now I have no choice but to like him. That son of a bitch.

He snatches the spray and the cloth, bringing it over to a cabinet in the corner. "Have a seat, ladies."

Karrie is still making eye contact with me, trying to get me to react all ooey-gooey like she is, but I remain stoic as I pull out a chair that has a box stuffed with files on it. I attempt to lift the box and grunt when I'm unsuccessful.

"Hey, Tom," I call. "Help me with this big box and show us what kind of muscles you got."

He turns to face us, his brows crashing over his eyes. "My name is Zack, actually."

I put a hand on my hip and stare at him. "So, muscles, or?"

He looks at Karrie, who looks mildly embarrassed, then shrugs and walks over to take the box off the chair. I'm a little mollified that he grunts under the weight of the box as he sort of shuffles over to his desk and drops it on the floor.

His face is a little red when he straightens, but he holds his hand toward the chair for me to sit, so I do.

"Where are we starting today?" Karrie asks with false cheer.

I glance at her to see if she's turned green yet in anticipation, but other than the lack of color in her cheeks, she seems okay for the moment.

TCT sits in his desk chair and wheels it forward to his fancy computer, scooting his microphone out of the way to give us a good view of his screen. "Well, I was thinking of maybe going through a John Doe list for areas where some of these dates of yours were last seen and maybe compare."

Well, damn, that's a good idea.

Karrie's shoulders fall a little, and I keep myself from reminding her how tedious investigative work really is. Especially because a little giddy thrill shoots through me at the prospect. Of course, I've kept my eyes out for any news of possible discovery of the men I've killed, but there were one or two names on Tom's list I wasn't aware of, so I'm curious to find out what else is going on here.

There are a lot of faces we sift through, and I can tell we're losing Karrie. Half the time, I'm the one who's responding, and I realize this is the only time True Crime Tom and I are legit vibing where he and Karrie are not. Because I love this stuff, and he clearly does too.

But even we lose steam after a while, and he's just mindlessly scrolling through pictures, and I'm thinking about what I want to make for dinner when a face catches my eye.

"Wait!" I grab his arm, accidentally making him slide past the picture I'd wanted a closer look at.

Karrie sits up and locks her phone, which she'd been scrolling through, doing some online shopping.

"Go back up," I say, holding back from taking the mouse from him and doing it myself. Because even though he cleaned his studio for me, I'd bet he's never thought to clean that—the thing he literally rubs his dirty man hands all over for hours at a time. Sneezing on his palms and going right back.

The image half-distracts me until the face comes back into view. I tilt my head, looking at the slightly deformed face. But I definitely think this could be Marcus.

Karrie makes a sort of choked sound behind me then leaps out of her chair, running for the bathroom. The sound of her retching is as much of a confirmation as her words would have been.

"You have any water? Or maybe some Seven-Up?" I frown, looking at Tom. His concerned gaze is glued on the closed door.

He jerks to look at me, but the concern doesn't leave his face, etching itself into the lines on his forehead. "I think I have some ginger ale..."

"I'll get it while you read me the report. It'll be better since she's out of the room."

He points to the fridge in the corner of the room, and spins to his computer, though he casts several looks toward the bathroom, his body tense like he'd rather go check on her than be the star amateur detective I know he is.

"Uh, John Doe located in a Mexican border town."

Makes sense given that we used to live in Austin, Texas.

"No ID or money—presumed stolen," Tom continues. "Looks like a mugging gone wrong. The state of his face is due to the beating he took."

I pop the tab on the ginger ale and knock softly on the door.

Karrie opens it, looking sheepish.

"Kar," is all I say.

She takes the can from me. "I'm fine."

She's always had a weak stomach. No roller coasters, no horror flicks, no donating blood. Hell, even winding mountain roads make her queasy. So it's not like this is a weird or unexpected reaction. But it still seems ill-advised that she'd keep pushing through on this scooby-dooing when it's clearly taking a toll.

"We don't have to keep doing this." I lower my voice so Tom can't hear. "I'm pretty sure he's as invested in proving you're innocent as you are."

She gives me a glare that's weakened by her watery eyes. "I've got it under control. Just, maybe we shouldn't look at dead bodies anymore?"

I shrug. "Seems fair."

She follows me cautiously back toward Tom, who scrolls away from the image and leaves only the text on the screen. He rubs a soothing hand up and down her arm in reassurance.

She smiles gratefully, tucking a chunk of black hair behind her ear. His eyes follow the movement, tracing her face with a hint of longing in his eyes.

"I think Zoe's right," Karrie says, gesturing at the computer with the ginger ale in her hand. "I'm pretty sure that's Marcus."

Tom looks confused at the turn of conversation for a second, and I roll my eyes that even a guy who seems as smart as he does can be dazzled by every little move Karrie makes. Not that she *isn't* straight up dazzling. But it's still astounding how stupid a guy can get over a woman of any caliber. Maybe because I've never been dazzled by anyone.

"Marcus?" TCT says, turning back around to pull out his notebook with the list of names. "Marcus Kennedy?"

"That's the one," I reply as Karrie takes a big gulp of her drink.

Tom writes something in his notebook in surprisingly not chicken scratch boy penmanship while I ponder. I hadn't even known Marcus was missing. Their fling had been good while it lasted. She'd pulled away a little when he'd seemed to want to get serious, and it had eventually led to a mutual, if not entirely amicable split, though she'd kept that on the down-low for a bit, even from me.

I think it had been harder on her than she'd expected, and she always seemed a little embarrassed that she couldn't commit to him, like she wondered if maybe her wandering eyes and heart said something about her when a nice guy was right in front of her.

I'd told her she didn't have to fit into any mold just because it "seemed" right, or she "should" have been happy or satisfied with it. Who the hell cared? Anyone who did was not an important person in her life anyway.

The timing and the suspicious nature of his death definitely nags at me though. Not because I actually believe she's cursed, but three guys dying in mysterious ways—and not by my hand—is too many to dismiss as coincidence.

So what exactly is going on?

This is going to make everything complicated because I want that answer, and I know True Crime Tom will be helpful in that area. But this puts me at risk of discovery as well.

Tom is looking at the screen and writing in his already crowded notebook, looking very much like the nerdy detective he is when his phone rings. He squints at it for a hot second, then his brows shoot up to his hairline.

"I gotta take this," he says, practically leaping from his chair and walking right out the front door.

"How we doing, Karrie?" I ask.

Her leopard print pointer finger picks at the tab on her soda can, making a *thwum* sound. Her dark eyes shift to mine. "This is seriously fucked up, Zoe. Like, what is happening?"

I grab her free hand and squeeze. "We'll figure it out."

Tom comes back into the room, his eyes shooting straight to Karrie, and he grimaces. "That was my contact down at the precinct. They just found a body down at the landfill."

Well, shit.

CHAPTER SEVEN

DEAD GIVEAWAY

D erek is dead.

It's fine. *It's fine, it's fine, it's fine.*

This is a little mantra I murmur to myself as I hang the last row of shirts in order from XXXL to XXS on the far wall of Bound by Fashion. The mantra I've been running through my mind for the past week as Zack, Zoe, and I continue our scooby-doo attempts—despite the fact that Zoe has taken to calling them "scooby-don'ts"— to figure out the swirling vortex of murder mystery surrounding my dating life.

Derek was awful. A piece of shit human being who had kiddie porn on his laptop.

Why he went on a date with me in the first place, I have no clue. I don't have any children in my life.

My stomach churns. Not at his death but at what he'd done in life. Actually, if I'm being honest with myself, there is a level of relief that he's dead and not just missing.

I frown at the realization. Definitely a note to keep to myself. It already looks bad enough that *another* guy I recently dated turned up dead.

Should I text Trent? Maybe warn him to double check his brakes before driving anywhere?

Sweat builds on my palms and brow. Trent sucked, but there's a huge gap between sucking and deserving of death.

I bend over, hands going to the rips in my pants just above my knees as I take some deep breaths. The list of men Zack has on his spreadsheet is longer than most people's entire dating life. I was relieved to see none of the list are any of the women I've dallied with. There haven't been many, I do prefer dick, but the occasional fellow busty goth girl catches my attention.

I shake away the dizziness that coats my vision for a moment. We are getting closer to an answer, narrowing down suspect lists—which Zack has kindly kept my name off of, though I'm sure he has a private murder board somewhere with red yarn attached to a bad picture of me.

I straighten and wipe away the beginning of tears, forcing myself not to cry—and not just because my make-up is impeccable right now.

Right on time, Zack pushes the front door open, sending a tinkling of bells through the store.

"Hungry?" he calls, knowing I'm in the back getting the last of the displays sorted before the next girl comes in for her shift.

"Starving." I plaster on a smile that warms into a real one when I catch sight of him. The last couple weeks have been a blur of information, but hearing most of it in his smooth rumble of a voice makes it all a bit more palatable.

Add on how good the man looks in a button up, and I'd be swooning if I wasn't worried about him being violently murdered for kissing me.

Not to mention part of him still thinking I'm a killer...

"Zoe with us tonight?" Zack asks as I stride behind the counter to grab my purse.

I nod. "Not till later though, she's got to wrap up a couple meetings. We have plenty of time to grab dinner first."

We stick around for a few minutes, waiting for Stacey to show for her shift. When she arrives I let her count out the register and then Zack and I head to a burger place we've become regulars at.

Zoe is a fan of the food but not the atmosphere. I order a to-go bag of garlic fries for her.

Talk flows easily. Zack likes giving details, part of the whole detective thing, and I enjoy hearing them. He's been telling me about the history of the city. He grew up here, knows all the ins and outs, and loves the place more than most.

He had an older brother, one who showed him the ropes and all the best places for teenagers to get into (and out of) trouble. Their parents were kind of like mine–not the best. They're third generation Malaysian-Americans and they veered hard away from the helicopter parent trope. Hard enough that they were closer to missing persons than actual parents. When Zack was fifteen, his brother was killed in a convenience store robbery gone wrong. He hadn't been involved, hadn't done anything wrong. Just a case of misfortune—wrong time and place. The hours Zack spent in the waiting room for his brother to come out of surgery alive only to be faced with the worst means he avoids hospitals like the plague.

Zack basically raised himself after that. Well, his numerous friends here helped.

I tentatively ask about his lovelife, and while I get confirmation on what I'd already sussed out—he's single—there is something in his expression when he shifts the conversation to me.

I tell him about Zoe's folks. Doc and Griller she calls them, I go with Mom and Dad, as they were essentially surrogate parents by the time I turned twelve. Zack laughs when I tell him about her nicknames for her own parents. He's gotten so used to "Tom" that he doesn't bat an eye when Zoe calls him by it.

We finish dinner, bag up the leftovers plus Zoe's meal, and head out to meet her. My phone beeps, and a flash of text from my bestie says she has to stay online for another thirty minutes to deal with an idiot. I chuckle as the update is followed by a string of profanity and angry emojis.

"Walk by the water while we wait?" Zack asks as he tucks the food on the floor in the back seat of his car.

I agree, ice cream on my mind, and we stroll down the street a bit until we reach the lake. I buy us each a scoop and we wander the path at a leisurely pace.

He shoots glances at me as we go, briefly at first, then he's basically staring sideways, and I worry he's about to run into a tree.

"Yes?" I chuckle, licking around the edge of my mint chip to stop it dripping.

He flushes and looks at his ice cream. His cheeks are almost as pink as the strawberry he ordered. "I like it when you do new stuff." Zack does a swirly gesture around his face.

It's my turn to flush, my face getting hot as I recall the spider nose ring I'm wearing. It matches a new stencil design I tried out on my cheekbone, as well as the new sparkly black mascara I just bought.

"Thanks." I gaze out onto the lake for somewhere to look besides him. There's something twisted with my brain. We've been studying the disgusting art of death for the last several weeks—which has led to me buying a stack of seltzers and several packages of saltines due to the copious amounts of vomiting—but I can't help the attraction.

"You know," he looks down at his ice cream, coming to a stop, "if 73.5 percent of the guys you date didn't end up missing or dead, I'd ask you on a propper one... try for something more than just being friends."

My heart does a full gold metal gymnast's floor routine. I'm frozen for a moment, then ice cream drips down onto my fingers, and I snap out of it.

"Yeah," I say with a grin. "And if some part of you didn't still suspect me of multiple murders, I'd say yes. I, uh, I don't want *you* to die."

He breaks into a laugh, and the tension hanging in the air blows away with the breeze.

"I take it you're fine with the outcome of some of the men from your past?"

A chill goes through me. We've talked a lot about my exes. Some were serious, some were flings, some were a single date followed by what I thought was me getting ghosted. Turns out, they were going missing.

"I don't know about *fine*." I lick a piece of chocolate out of my molar. "But part of me is a bit relieved about some of them not being around to hurt anyone else."

His smile drops. "Who?"

"Vincent." I brush back a lock of hair like this is a casual conversation. Like I don't have spiders crawling through my gut.

"He's the first one on the list. The one who was good at gaslighting."

I nod. "He would be. I had maybe three dates before we started going out, and they were all with other guys freshman year of high school."

"So first serious boyfriend."

A low rumble of embarrassment surges in my chest. "Yeah. It was the start of Junior year of high school."

I feel Zack's gaze but don't look at him.

"I know how dumb that is. He was way older, lived alone, and was exactly the kind of guy you'd expect to go for high school girls. But he was really sweet at first. Gave me all the attention in the world, literally a gift every day when he'd walk me home from school."

Zoe informed me later that this is known as *love-bombing*. It's a tactic used by abusive individuals to lure someone into the cycle of abuse. It endears the victim to the abuser. At the time, neither of us had the language for the concept..

An itch prickles the back of my neck. Zack doesn't say anything, leaving me to fill the silence with more of the story.

"We got serious really quick. You know my parents weren't super there. Zoe's place was always home, but with Vincent, it felt like the place was mine too. He did dumb stuff that felt really special at the time, like freeing up a drawer for me."

I roll my eyes at younger-me's naivety.

This was also the timeframe that he got jealous of any time I spent time with Zoe or anyone else. He used the example of the drawer as a way to keep me with him. *"Zoe's parents didn't give you a drawer, did they?"*

"I was on the fast track for Berkely."

At this, Zack's even footsteps falter.

I grimace. "Yeah, surprising to me too. But I was going to go into sociopolitics. Instead, I moved in with Vincent a few days before I turned eighteen. He told me he needed me there. He said we'd go when we had a little more money saved up. He'd support me through school."

My free hand clenches, and it feels like a bad idea to be holding ice cream right now. "That was all bullshit. He isolated me from everyone." A smile splits my melancholy. "Everyone except Zoe, that is. She was in that apartment every Wednesday for movie night, no matter how many times I told her not to come."

I fall into silence for a moment, contemplating what my existence might be now if Zoe hadn't kept her pink stiletto in the doorframe of my life. She refused to budge, refused to leave when Vincent got loud, refused to take my words to heart when I told her neither of us wanted her there.

Because she knew it wasn't true. She knew it was Vincent, knew he had some deep claws into me. His barely concealed antagonism (and the way he'd block her from coming in) must have told her more than she needed to know. Add to that the way I had become a shell of myself, and she knew there was a major problem.

It was the only time I ever said anything like that to her, and it was my biggest regret to this day. But I don't say any of this to Zack.

"How did you get away from him?" Zack asks after I'm quiet a little too long.

I swallow. "He uh... he went past yelling. For a long time when he hit something, that something was the wall. He'd throw things, break dishes, slam doors hard enough to crack." A shudder of fury runs down my spine. It had felt like I had no one. I'd called the police the first time he'd gone too far with his aggression, but they'd said there was nothing they could do. Not until he actually hurt me. When he did escalate, I didn't bother calling them. "At a point, that wasn't enough. That's when I walked out."

Zack exhales a long breath. "That's really... well, it's not easy to get away from something like that. That was really brave of you."

I snort, a derisive sound that's ruder than I mean it to be. "I appreciate that. Anyway, a week of banging on Zoe's parents door, and several threats of calling the cops, he finally left me alone. Moved, in fact. After that, things were done. He was gone. When Zoe left for college, she brought me with her."

"It sounds like he took a lot from you."

I shrug as though Vincent didn't steal nearly everything I cared about. My grandmother's necklace to pawn for rent. My 'promising' future. My innocence. And that was before he'd moved. When he left, he took the only happy pictures from my childhood, a collection of stuffed pigs from a decade of summer fairs with Zoe's family, and the matching bracelet she made me all those years ago—little elephants like hers, but mine were black. It was gone when he was, packed up with all his shit and moved to whatever podunk town he ended up in. I never got any of it back.

But I don't tell Zack about that either. I let the silence take over as we make our trek around the lake back to the car. My mint chocolate chip still tastes fine, but the cold of it leaves a pit in my stomach. I need something warm tonight.

My cheeks flush, and I dart a glance at Zack, whose expression is marred in seriousness.

Hot chocolate. I'll get some hot chocolate tonight with Zoe after we finish our scooby session.

I pluck at the edge of my shirt. "So, anything on your end in that way?"

He glances at me with a confused furrow. "What do you mean?"

I shrug. "Any horrible exes?"

He lets out half a laugh, but it sounds pained. "I've had my share of bad breakups." He raises and drops a shoulder. The muscles in his back are tight. "Nothing worth talking about."

I let it end with that, but his jaw is clenched for a long moment as we make our way back to the car.

"Seriously, though," Zack murmurs as we both lean in to toss the ends of our cones into the garbage can on the street, "when we find out what's going on, do you want to go for it?"

I swallow down the fear that bubbles up in my throat. Fear for him, since I'm cursed to be the end of three quarters of the men I date. And fear for me, because putting my heart on any kind of line keeps ending with it getting crushed.

I force a smile and wipe my sticky fingers with one of the wet wipes Zack keeps in his car. "Ask me when we've solved the case."

I hop in, close the door, and am deeply focused on my phone by the time he climbs into the driver's seat.

My feelings for Zack are plastered on my face when Zoe arrives. At least, it feels that way with the knowing stare she gives me.

I ignore the look, hand over her food, and settle into my corner of the room with a notebook at the ready. Notes—that's where I shine in this equation. With Zack and Zoe not wanting me to catch a glimpse of a body on the computer screen, I'm often relegated to the little round table.

To my surprise, Zoe settles across from me and lays out her dinner. I cock my head, one eyebrow raised.

"What?" She glares. "I'm hungry."

I keep my lips shut but give her a smirk. My surprise has nothing to do with her chowing down on lukewarm fries, and everything to do with how comfortable she must be in Zack's studio for her to be okay eating here.

Another reason to like a guy I *cannot* continue falling for.

I heave a sigh, catching a glance from them both before Zack gets us started.

"Okay." He stretches his neck, cracks his fingers, and settles into his seat before the computer. "We have several bodies now."

I scrawl names in a list down my paper. *Derek, Marcus, David, Logan, Vincent.* An odd set of very different men. Vincent had been a prick and a lowlife. David and I had met at his cousin's wedding. We had fun, but I thought he'd fully ghosted me after we went back to our respective cities. Logan wasn't a bad guy, just a beach bum with basically no priorities. Marcus was a sweetie, someone a normal girl could settle down with. Derek was a pedophile.

Zack says basically the same thing, minus the bit about dating. Try as we might, none of us can find a connection between these men... besides me.

We switch gears for a bit, listing out the missing men, comparing them once again to John Does in the database I'm not a hundred percent sure Zack has permission to be in.

I avoid that part, my gaze sliding to the box of manilla folders as the other two scan pictures of dead people. My stomach hasn't allowed me to get far in that field. But I haven't tried regular crime scene photos—ones without bloody corpses in the picture.

A metallic taste fills my mouth, and I blink hard, swallowing down the nausea stirring in my gut.

I pull forth the first folder: Derek. He was found in the landfill, packaged in a garbage bag. A chuckle pulls from my chest; the landfill is an appropriate place for trash to end up.

I'm careful as I open the folder, quickly flipping over the images with his partially dismembered corpse. The street where they picked up the load that included him is unfamiliar to me. Nothing about the fancy houses, white picket fences, and overly manicured lawns stirs any epiphany. Next is the landfill itself. A cop is in the midst of shoo-ing a seagull off the Gladbag Derek was found in.

Purposefully avoiding the fact that a body is spilling out the opposite side of the bag, I focus on the details. I recognize the brand. It's a fragrance one, cherry, with a pink drawstring. We've been using them for years. Zoe *hates* the plastic smell of regular trash bags.

I move on to Marcus, but I've never been to the border town he was found in. Nothing rings any bells for me.

Logan wasn't even on the cop's radar. He drowned in a river not far off the coast. I suppose that is suspicious to me though; the man was a serious swimmer. Like, no drinking or getting high before getting in the ocean type of swimmer. Surfing was his life; it seems unlikely that he'd die in what looks like a pretty shallow creek.

Flipping on, I get to David. The cops spent a while on him. I shouldn't be surprised no one in the family contacted me. It was only a week, after all. His car was found at the start of a mountain pass. It had rolled many times. He'd died quickly. Eventually it was ruled an accident. Faulty brakes.

My chest tightens.

Something about the last couple weeks of doing this makes thinking about their deaths less impactful. This must be how cops feel. They're able to disconnect from the horror enough to think through the clues. I'm not quite there yet—the thought of bloody, mangled bodies has me diving for my purse and coming back up with a stick of minty gum. Something to keep my mouth moving while I avoid gross pictures.

Last and least... Vincent.

I flip past the first several pictures, though I could probably slow down on them; Vincent was found so long after his death, he almost blended into the background in the quarry where he was dumped.

I chew furiously on the gum, inhaling through my nose.

"Hey." Zoe glances over at me. Her eyebrow arches. "You good?"

I nod.

She purses her lips. "Don't look at those, Kar. If you throw up, I'm gonna insist we go home."

Zack chuckles. "The seltzer is in the minifridge if you need some."

"Thanks." I give a tightlipped smile and take him up on the offer. Popping the tab, I settle back in as my friends return to their research. They've finally exhausted John Does and have switched to referencing bodies and missing persons with a few different sets of maps.

I flip the last body photo over and study the wide angled image of the quarry. It's far enough that I can't make out the body. Nothing helpful. Next is a street. Odd.

I squint, and pull the picture closer. Dusk, or maybe dawn, and it looks like this was taken by some kind of security camera. Maybe from a shop.

I flip the pic and note a scrawling across the bottom: *Suspect?*

I turn it back over and look closer. There isn't anyone in the image, just a row of cars parked along a clean-looking sidewalk. A few trees, their leaves shedding and landing on the top of a white sedan at the very edge of the image.

I lean in. Is there someone in that car?

No. It's a reflection in the window. Someone walking along the sidewalk, just out of frame.

I reach for the magnifying glass Zoe and I spent a good thirty minutes teasing Zack over the first time he pulled it out. The torso in the reflection is muddled, but the person's wrist is visible. Early morning light makes it hard to distinguish very much color. Is that a bracelet?

My nose is nearly touching the table. The bracelet is black, little charms dangling from the bottom. An inch above, the fringe of a vibrant pink sleeve is just visible.

I freeze.

My insides go numb as my mind catches up with my eyes. I've stopped breathing.

I look again, giving a little disbelieving shake of my head as I confirm what my eyes are telling me they see.

This isn't possible.

I swallow, my throat tight, my lungs aching.

Inhale. That's right. Breathe, don't forget to breathe.

I know that bracelet. A matching one dangles above the shoe rack in my apartment. I know the sweater. I've picked it up from the dry cleaners more times than I can count.

Memories rip through me.

"Don't forget to pick up more trash bags. We're almost out."

"We need new knives. Those ones aren't good anymore."

"Can you pick up my lucky sweater..."

I'm breathing now. Too hard. Too fast.

One of the others makes a sound, and I lurch. My arm knocks the seltzer, and it clatters to the ground, sticky fuzzy liquid seeps out onto the carpet.

Zack and Zoe spin to look at me.

My eyes are wide, fear holding me so tight I don't know how to break free.

"Karrie," Zack asks, concern laced across his expression. "Are you okay?"

Hesitation clutches me for the briefest of moments. Then I nod. "I just started my period."

He mouths like a horrified fish.

I turn my gaze onto Zoe. "We need to go."

She hesitates, worry taking hold of her in a way only I can evoke. "Okay, we can go. Tom, want to pick this up next time?"

He glances at the screen, and I take the opportunity to fold the picture between my trembling fingers.

"Yeah," he begins.

I dart from the table, snatch my purse off the chair, and grab Zoe's arm.

She stares with alarmed eyes.

"We need to go."

Without another word, because I don't trust myself not to either vomit dinner or a confession, I drag my best friend, my sister, the one person I care about most in the world, out of Zack's studio.

I stumble a bit down the steps, and Zoe is there to catch me. Like she always is.

My head spins.

We burst from the side door of the cute little bookstore Zack works over. The sun is gone, night chilling the air and sending another wave of shivers down my spine.

I release Zoe's arm when we reach the car, let her climb into the passenger's seat, and stalk around to the driver's side.

It's only after I've shut and locked the doors and made sure the windows are rolled up that I face my friend.

My heart can't keep beating this fast. There's no way it's healthy.

I inhale, exhale, and inhale again.

Zoe watches me, those calm eyes infuriating as my world crashes down around me. A long moment passes while I try to figure out how to start the words. The crumpled picture incriminating her is still clenched in my fist.

Then Zoe sighs, flips her hair, and squirts some hand sanitizer into her palm. "So, what gave it away?"

Chapter Eight

BODY COUNT

In hindsight, I probably shouldn't have let Karrie drive. Not only is she practically hyperventilating, I am *very* concerned her eyes are going to bulge so hard they'll pop out of her head.

"How many, Zoe?"

Oooh, that's a weird growly sound I've never heard in her voice before. But then I realize maybe it's because she's fighting her stomach's urge to upchuck her dinner. Which I can appreciate. I might love Karrie more than anyone in the world, but I don't relish the idea of her vomit anywhere near me.

I purse my lips and fold my hands in my lap. "Uh, how many is too many?"

Her face jerks to me so fast, it's like exorcist-level creepy. "One, Zoe. One is too many."

Got it. So no winning here. But I wonder if maybe I can soften the blow a bit, vague-up my answers. "We're still in the single digits."

Finger guns are probably not the best punctuation in this scenario, but I don't realize that in time to stop myself.

If possible, her eyes go bigger, and she looks back at the road. Her hands twist on the steering wheel and the jerky way she makes the turns back toward our apartment tell me that my job as bodyguard might end tonight in a fiery inferno of twisted metal and broken glass.

Definitely should have insisted on driving.

"I can't believe you killed him."

I'm not sure which files she was looking at when the realization hit, but I'm guessing it was either Vincent or Derek since they're the only two of mine whose bodies have turned up.

Asking "which him" is probably a bad idea, so I just flatten my mouth and tap my thumbs against each other.

"You killed Vincent!"

Ah, okay. That "him."

I nod. "Yeah. But he was going to kill you."

Her brows crash down over her eyes as she thinks that through.

She might not have seen it, but she had still been tied up in the cycle of abuse. But I could see it plain as day. Especially with the way he'd come around my parents' and bang on the door. I never let her go anywhere alone because I knew he was out there. I'd discovered him quietly stalking a few times. And he was not one to give up. I could feel it. After some digging, I found out he'd bought a gun and considered the gut feeling confirmed.

I didn't go full knife mode right away, though. I called the police, told them the story, and informed them he had a gun. As had happened with Karrie the first time Vincent had thrown his fist through a wall, they couldn't do anything. He had the correct paperwork and no priors. So, I took care of it myself.

"*You* killed him," she whispers at the dashboard.

I blink. "Because he was going to kill *you*."

She looks at me. "You *killed* him."

I look behind me as if there's a camera crew for a prank reality show. There isn't. "Yep. I sure did." I speak this part slower: "Because he was going to kill you."

She just keeps staring at me. "And Derek."

"Trashbag Douchebag. Yep. Did him too."

She slams her hands on the steering wheel.

"Do you want me to drive?" I ask in a quiet voice.

She just shoots a fiery glare at me. It's just as well. We're only a couple of blocks away from our place.

Silence blankets the cab of the car, and I decide not to break it. I won't answer a question unless she asks. Honestly, the less she knows, the better. Not just because of her stomach issues. But for her safety if the cops ever come knocking on our door.

I went into the killing business fully aware of what could happen to me if I ever get caught (though I have been incredibly careful to keep that from happening). But I would never want her to go down with me.

The whole point was to keep her safe. It's why I had to keep her bracelet all these years. Because damn right I took it back from Vincent. But as much as I wanted to return it to her, that would open up a line of questioning I didn't want to get into. It would have pulled her into the mess I was trying to keep her out of.

We pull into our designated parking spot, and she stomps her way to our front door, squeezing the car keys in her hand like she wants to stab me with them.

I don't offer to help as she unsuccessfully tries to stick the key in the lock, then follow her inside once she finally gets it. I shut the door quietly behind me and move toward the kitchen.

"Seltzer?" I offer.

She shoots me a look full of incredulity as she starts pacing the living room, her nostrils flared.

So I shrug and pull out the wine I always keep on hand for myself. She's a cocktail girl, generally, so the wine is usually left for me to finish. But as soon as I finish pouring my glass, she snatches it off the counter and chugs it.

I press my lips together and go to retrieve another glass to fill for myself.

"So Vincent and Derek," she finally says, her voice feeling harsh against the brittle silence. She puts down her empty glass with more force than necessary, and I briefly worry about it breaking.

But I wisely keep my mouth shut as I take a sip of my wine, watching her over the rim of the glass.

She stops pacing and puts her hands on her hips. "Who else, Zoe?"

I lift a shoulder and make a face. I'm really not sure she's ready for the rest.

"Adam Delaney?" she demands.

"Handsy Harry," I correct, and she knows this is confirmation.

"What did he do?"

I have clever nicknames, but they're fairly self-explanatory. "Um, he was handsy."

She narrows her eyes. "And that's a crime?"

"Not with you, maybe. Though I'd argue unwanted and unsolicited manhandling wouldn't sit right with you either."

She pulls her head back. "Okay, fair. But murder, Zoe? Really?"

"Um, Handsy Harry had moved to the darkside when it came to getting handsy." I tip my glass and look into the red depths of the liquid. "He strangled a girl and nearly killed her."

Karrie gasps, drawing my gaze.

"And it wasn't the first time." Nor the least deadly. A case had been dropped against him with the same accusation—strangulation, though the girl had later died. It was unclear how he got out of charges. One thing was clear, and this is what I decide to share with Karrie: "Consent was dubious, at best."

Her hands go to her mouth, and her pale face tells me this may be enough information for now.

"I know this is a lot, but maybe we should call it a night and sleep on it," I suggest.

She nods, rubbing at her temples. She did down that wine pretty quickly. It always messes with her more than other kinds of alcohol, but at least it will probably help her sleep.

I put my arm around her shoulders and guide her down the hall to her room. It's a win that she doesn't flinch away from my touch. She must know that she's in no danger from me, though that fear has crossed my mind once or twice.

A killer is a killer.

Two Days Later

"Jeremy Hicks?!"

The topic didn't come up again for a while, though Karrie has been walking around our apartment a little dazed. I figure she's been putting pieces together in her mind and studying the list of names we have of missing or dead dudes. Sure as hell she didn't remember all of their names.

Then this morning, she was almost back to her chipper self, putting her makeup on with careful precision as usual, curling her dark locks with the red and purple dyed streaks, and singing along to whatever song plays on the radio. Because she does still listen to the radio.

But then she marches into the living room while I'm booting up my computer to get started on work, and the first thing out of her mouth is Reject Richard's name in a comically incredulous tone.

"Beat women when they rejected his advances," I reply calmly, setting up my webcam for the two chunks of time today that I will need to be in virtual meetings.

She stomps back down the hall in bare feet, probably to rage-put-on socks since she's going to wear her combat boots to the boutique today. I know because she has very specific outfits planned out that go with specific pairs of shoes.

Our preference in styles might be polar opposites, but Karrie really knows how to do hers with flair and in a way that is more model-like than just straight goth. And on top of that, I am well-acquainted with what combinations she thinks look best.

One Day Later

Karrie practically flings herself into the apartment, her hair flowing wildly around her shoulders as her eyes zero in on me.

I pause my movie and set the remote next to my untouched bowl of popcorn on the coffee table, ready for her to throw another name at me. I'd been done with work for a couple of hours already, but the store doesn't close until seven, so I made the popcorn for both of us and have been waiting for her.

"David Van Zuiden?!"

She says this while still carefully taking her boots off and setting them neatly on the shoe rack, which warms my heart. Either the habit is way too ingrained or she really does love me despite my—ahem—wayward tendencies.

I click my tongue. "Actually, that one wasn't me."

She freezes in the act of hanging her jacket on its peg. "Wait." She brushes her fingers across the bracelet hung above the shoe rack and then spins slowly to look at me.

I raise my brows. "I didn't even know who that guy was."

At this, her eyes dart away. We don't often keep secrets from each other, but since I have been keeping a real big one, I let it slide that I didn't know about this guy and that she clearly feels guilty about the fact.

"He was the wedding date guy." She moves farther into the room, picking absently at the fringe of the ripped jeans she's wearing. You can see her fishnets peeking through the holes.

"Ah." Okay, so she did tell me about him. It was a destination wedding for one of her friends, a week-long deal in the Hamptons. She'd met a guy, of course, because it's her. They had a whirlwind romance she genuinely thought would extend past the wedding week.

She'd never given me a name, so I hadn't really done any digging, but he'd ghosted her afterwards anyway, so it became moot.

"His brakes were faulty, wasn't that what Zack said?" She sits next to me on the couch.

"Yeah, that's not my style."

She looks at me, much less sharply than I would expect. "What is your style?"

I grimace. "Do you really want to know?" Because stab-by-stabby, blood spurting, and dismemberment isn't what I'd call a safe topic for Karrie's poor traumatized digestive system.

"Knives, right?" she asks softly.

I click my teeth together and don't confirm. Because I'm still holding out for her to keep plausible deniability when it comes to having a serial killer as a best friend.

"What are you watching?" she asks instead of pushing.

"Pride & Prejudice & Zombies." Which is *definitely* not her style. "But we can watch the regular one. I was just waiting for you." I point to the popcorn bowl, and she sighs, picking it up and flopping back against the couch.

Two Days Later

"Jackson Rojas?"

I've gotten used to our routine, so it doesn't surprise me enough to stop what I'm doing, which is finishing up a sudoku instead of anything work-related.

I nod. "Puppy Puncher."

She's got half her makeup done, so she looks a little odd with crazy thick eyeliner and no lashes done or any added color to her face. It makes her look like she's all eyeballs and nothing else. "What does that mean?"

"He killed puppies. He was a psycho."

She clicks her tongue and thrusts out a hip. "Like you?"

I scoff and lean back in my chair. "Excuse me. I would never hurt a puppy."

"No, you're just a fucking serial killer."

I tap my pen against my chin. "I like to consider myself a vigilante. I kill in the name of justice. Like Batman."

She pouts. "Batman didn't kill people."

"Didn't he?" I challenge, though I don't actually know. "You're murdering people, Zoe."

I sigh, setting my pen down. Yes, I absolutely do sudoku in pen. Because I rarely make a mistake. "Can you honestly say the world isn't a better place without these douchebags in it?"

She thinks on it, looking grudgingly like she might agree. "What about Marcus?"

Judging by her subdued tone, I'd guess she already knows this answer. "Considering I've never been to Mexico and he was found beaten and robbed of his IDs and money, that has none of my usual flair."

"What flair is that?"

"With the exception of Derek, the bodies never get found. And that was just some bad luck."

Who knew the fancy block I'd left Trashbag Douchebag was the same one where some big wig politician lived? He'd cheated on his wife, and she'd thrown out a bunch of his very sentimental-slash-expensive stuff the same night as retribution.

And of course, Big Wig *had* to send some hired hands out to dig through the trash in the landfill to look for it it. But what they found was Derek Waters. I have no idea if they found whatever Big Wig had actually been looking for. But regardless, it would be seized as part of their evidence until they could rule them out as connected.

Maybe things would spin in my favor, and they'd blame the death on said Big Wig, and this whole mess would disappear. But I'm not going to hold my breath.

"So you didn't kill David or Marcus..." Her face scrunches up.

"Or Surf Bro," I add.

She gives me a skeptical look.

I hold up my hands. "Listen, no more secrets. I'll share any detail you want. But those guys weren't me. And their deaths weren't even obviously murder. But the fact that they all mysteriously died not long after dating you is sus-picious to me. Which means I'm even more in this than before."

She narrows her eyes at me. "Were you in this just to keep us off your trail?"

I've sworn not to keep any more secrets, so I sigh. "Yes. And to keep my eye on Tom since you're obviously smitten with him." I scoot forward in my chair and place my hands on my knees. "It's become more though. Those guys who've died—not because of me—are shooting up some serious red flags."

"Red flags, Zoe?"

"Okay. I get it." I stand up so that she and I are almost eye-to-eye (almost because I'm taller). "Karrie, I'm really sorry. Not about the dead guys, obviously. Douchebags deserve a rough end. But I *am* sorry I didn't tell you about any of it. Honestly, I was trying to protect you. In case..." I nibble my lip for a second because a fear that didn't plague me before now is. "In case I got caught or something. I didn't want to take you down with me."

Her shoulders slump and she leans forward to throw her arms around my waist. I hug her back, glad that she's willing to forgive me.

She gives a watery laugh against my shoulder. "That is the sweetest, most twisted thing anyone has ever said to me."

"Love you."

"Love you back."

A Debt Owed

Dissociating appears to be one of the many skills I didn't know I had until I needed it. Along with being able to fix fishnets stockings, parallel park, and quickly calculate a tip in my head, it's come in handy lately.

I stride into Bound by Fashion and switch registers with the girl who had the morning shift. It'll be a quiet day, middle of the week and all.

I'll be left to my thoughts.

Zoe has murdered people. People, the plural of person, more than one, more—probably—than she's telling me. Though her forthrightness has been lightly startling, vomit-inducing, and greatly appreciated.

I'm getting past the death part, though I think I've lost a few pounds from being unable to hold down food at the sight of our pink trash bags, or Zoe chopping up veggies for a stir-fry. (Yes, I still ate the stir-fry. She's a crazy good cook.)

Her answers for each man she's killed have been… more than satisfactory. I've been having nightmares since the day I figured it out. More each time I learn another disturbing truth about one of the men I dated.

Vincent, coming back to Zoe's house like he did so many times after I left. In my dreams, he does more than slam on the door and scream through the windows. In my dreams, the puppy puncher has the time to graduate to killing. In my dreams, Derek uses me as a convenient cover for his horrific predilections.

Each time I wake, panting for breath with sheets tangled around my legs and fear gripping me tight, I'm comforted by the realization that none of them can hurt anyone else. Ever again.

Batman's whole thing about killing makes you a killer… feels like it doesn't apply to Zoe. Even if the emotional side of me *was* still in hysterics, logic says she's stopped a fair amount of brutality and a handful of deaths—including mine.

So yeah, I'm not too mixed up over the murder part anymore.

Though my heart sinks as I realize Zack and I can't have a future together while he's got a secret about his past. I can't fathom him doing something that would prompt Zoe to 'take care of him', but I won't risk it. Not with him being so cagey about whatever it is he doesn't want to talk about.

I flash a smile as the bell at the front rings. An older woman comes in, a teenager trailing behind with low interest.

I let them know I'm here to help, and then go back to rearranging the bracelets on display.

No, it's not the murders that have my stomach still knotted into pieces. It's the fact that Zoe never told me.

It's an absolutely insane thing for me to be upset about; I've kept my share of secrets from Zoe. Granted, none of them come with twenty-five-to-life if anyone else finds out, but still... Part of me hates that she never told me. Hates that she never felt safe enough to keep me in the loop about the absolute shit human beings I've dated.

I shake my head, switching to earrings as frustration heats my gut. It feels stupid to be upset about it. She's been protecting me since we were kids. From assholes on the playground who didn't like my dark hair, who thought poking fun at the kid with dirty clothes was a good move. She proved them wrong time and again, usually with a cutting line that sent them crying to the teachers.

From the neglect of my family. How many nights would I have gone without eating if she hadn't dragged me to her house for dinner? How many lunches did she split in half to share before her mom started sending an extra one just for me?

She's always been there for me.

How many times have I been there for her?

My heart lurches just as the woman calls, "Excuse me, miss."

I jerk around and hurry over to help them style a handful of outfits. The teenager, maybe fourteen with braided brown hair and a baggy sweater, seems happy with the vibe we're able to create. The clothes will accentuate her height, the colors will bring tone to her pale skin, and I even talk her grandma into going for a few light shades of lipgloss.

A handful of customers come and go during my five-hour shift. I help them all with a bright smile. Inside, I'm all twisted up thinking about how much Zoe has done for me and how little I've given in return.

It's never been a transactional friendship or anything, but damn... how do you get to twenty-nine with a serial killer best friend who's murdered people for you and not be able to name a time you've done something remotely close to giving back?

I don't like takers. Part of why I don't make it through a lot of relationships. I refuse to be one.

So, when my shift is up, I vow to do something nice for Zoe.

I close up shop, make sure to turn off the lights and lock the place down, and then head over to the late night dry cleaners she uses for most of her clothes. I usually swing by to get things for her, but this time I'm aiming higher.

The windows are lit, a happy yellowing sign advertising their stain remover services. I push open the door and have a brief moment of hesitation. I'm not the only customer coming in so late.

A decently tall man I recognize stands in the corner, his brown hair swept back like he's brushed a hand through it too many times. I'm immediately comparing it to Zack's black cut, his darker skin, brighter eyes.

I shake that away, flashing a smile. "Hey. Connor, right? I've seen you here a few times."

He grins and nods, reaching out a hand. "Yeah, Karrie?"

I incline my head, flipping a lock of hair over my shoulder and stepping to the counter. I hand over the slip for Zoe's dresses, then lean in and inquire about my present. Lilia, the petite Italian woman who runs the place, raises an eyebrow at me and gives a number. I agree, and she shrugs.

As she moves away to collect my things, I turn back to Connor. "You're here a lot."

"You too." He steps forward, leaning on the counter with a kind but somewhat bland smile.

I force a chuckle. "My roommate has a lot of delicate clothes. She prefers dry cleaners to our regular laundry."

"Probably better for panty hose."

My brain runs a confused buzzing for a second, then Connor gestures to my legs. I've got on my favorite pair of fishnet stockings beneath a checkerboard skirt (it has pockets).

"Oh." This time the chuckle is real. "Fishnets. I actually wash all these in the sink."

My cheeks go pink as humor lights his face.

"I, uh, yeah. I've got to have all my shirts pressed for work, so..."

I give him a moment, waiting for more. He seems a bit stuck, so I toss a line.

"Where do you work?"

"I'm in finance," he says with a bobbing nod. "Pays well, decent hours, and I can take a good amount of time off during the year."

"That's nice." I glance behind the counter to see if Lilia is coming back with my things yet. No sign. "Do you travel much?"

He nods again, pulling his phone out as he steps beside me and flipping through a handful of pictures of a blurry figure snowboarding. "I get to the slopes as much as I can."

"That sounds nice," I say, cringing internally at the amount of times I've said nice in this conversation. I inhale, the smell of cleaning chemicals almost cleansing my mind.

I can't live my life afraid to date people. Zack is... off-limits for the time being. That thing he doesn't want to talk about from his past is scary enough, even without the Zoe factor. But add on the fact that he's actively looking for a killer, and I've got to keep him from finding out it's Zoe. Which means keeping him at a distance no matter how much I like him.

Relationships are hard enough, let alone trying to start one with all that going on.

"What?" I snap to attention, staring up at Connor after the realization that he's still talking, and I've grasped none of it.

"I was just... you don't have to, of course, but if you wanted to check out the lodge sometime, or just grab a drink or something."

"Oh." I grin. "Yeah, that'd be n—awesome."

I give him my number just as Lilia returns with both our orders. I heft the jug of 30% hydrogen peroxide, sling a set of dresses and sweaters over my arm, and follow Connor outside.

He holds the door with his free hand, dangling a set of almost identical beige shirts in the other.

I thank him with a smile.

"So, I'll call you sometime?" His voice is so hopeful it pulls a bit of my old self from the last few weeks of weird.

I run my tongue along my teeth and give an inviting grin. "Sounds great."

He stares after me as I walk to the car a few blocks down. The street is dark now, the sky a beautiful shade of blue. I soak in the growing chill in the air.

Sweater weather is on the way.

"I'm not saying you guys have to fall in love with him," I whine. "But I *need* you both to meet him. I've dated too many shitheads to trust myself anymore."

On the couch in front of me, Zack and Zoe are clearly holding back the urge to jailbreak themselves out of my request.

Tough luck for them; I'm the one holding the pizza.

"Karrie," Zack starts. "He sounds like a nice guy, but I have zero interest in spending time with him."

I grimace at the word nice. "I get that, but the two of you are joining us for dinner next week."

"What if we've already vetted him?" Zoe asks, her voice mild.

Zack nods, gesturing as though this will get him out of it. "Yeah, what if we watch the date or something?"

Zoe cocks her head at Zack, a scornful smile on her lips. "You want to what?"

He slaps his forehead into his palm. "That came out wrong."

Zoe cackles. "Yeah it did. Anyway." She turns to me. "No part of me is down to go eat with someone whose table manners might well cause me to vomit into my napkin."

I open my mouth, close it, and stomp my foot a little. With my free hand, I waft the closed and still-hot pizza box in their direction. "Let me make this simple. You both join me and Connor for a short dinner date, or you don't eat tonight."

Zoe turns to Zack, ignoring me entirely. "You know, we could just order another pizza. Seems easier than going to dinner with Captain Bland."

I groan as Zack's laugh splits the air.

He catches my eye, and I give him a pleading expression. With a sigh, he stands and takes the pizza from my hand. "I won't speak for Zoe, cuz I like my tongue in one piece, but I'll go to this dinner."

I light up, and he holds up a finger.

"Once. I'll meet this guy once."

I nod, all smiles, and then turn to Zoe.

She glares at Zack. "Traitor."

He shrugs and moves into the kitchen for plates. "I'm hungry," he calls back.

Zoe crosses her arms and frowns up at me. "Fine. But this counts as our weekly exploration of the city."

"Deal."

We join Zack in the kitchen, pile pizza onto our plates, and settle in for a Psych marathon.

Maybe an hour in, and I turn to Zoe as her words from earlier click into place. "Did you already look into Connor?"

Her eyes widen, but she doesn't look away from the screen. "Maybe."

My shoulders tense. "And...?"

Zack leans forward, meeting my eye across Zoe. "He's clean."

Zoe and I do a simultaneous eyebrow raise as we turn to look at him. There is a pause. I click the remote to halt the TV.

"What does that mean?" I demand.

Zoe snorts and leans back, her expression lightly snooty. "It means he's lacking any deep, dark secrets."

I scooch to the edge of the couch so I have a view of both of them. "I'm sorry. Did you *both* already vet the guy I'm seeing?"

Zack gives an incredulous chuckle. "It was that or take the risk that he's wanted for assault in another county."

"Or secretly a pedophile."

I cringe. Then I give my chin a thoughtful stroke. "Okay... so what did you find out?"

"Graduated high school in Omaha with a 3.97 GPA," Zoe says.

"Played football," Zack adds.

"But not well enough to take it to college."

"Cuma Sum Laud at Chicago State, but he couldn't handle the big city." Zack rolls his eyes at Zoe.

"Got his degree in business, then went back home for a few years," Zoe says with a stifled grin. "Worked at some finance office until his parents passed. They left him the house."

"He sold it, used the cash to move out here and has been working at Flint and Commons in their financial advisory office for the past four years."

I stare from one to the other, lightly horrified and rather impressed.

They're not done.

"Five-foot-eleven." Zoe gives Zack a playful glare.

"Thirty-three years old." Zack returns it before looking back at me.

"No family."

"Left field on his work kickball team."

"Paid his taxes three weeks early for the last four fiscal–"

"*Enough*!" I throw my hands up in exasperation. "I get it; you're both stupid good at sleuthing. Did he *kill* anyone? Does he hurt animals? Is he going to use me as a cover to become a supervillain?"

"Supervillan, no," Zoe says. "Captain Bland, yes."

Zack snorts.

I glare at them both, click the remote to turn Psych back on, and retreat to the kitchen for a glass of wine.

Connor brings me roses. A bit basic but sweet. They've got a black satin ribbon around them.

"Thanks." I flash a grin, untying the ribbon and pressing the middle of it to my throat. "Tie it for me?"

He hesitates, then it clicks and he hurries behind me to fix my new choker in place. I'm dressed to impress, a short black dress, satin red leggings with lips to match. He cleaned up well, though it's hard to say I've ever seen him not cleaned up. His suit is black, the shirt underneath white and buttoned nearly to the top. Safe date attire.

I smell the roses, then bring Connor inside so I can quickly clip and put them in a vase. He takes in the apartment, from the bracelet hanging on the wall to the pictures in the living room depicting over a decade of friendship.

"Your roommate?" He gestures to a picture of the two of us before we moved to Washington.

"Yeah." I grin at the post-eye-roll expression on Zoe's face in the picture. "She's who we are going to dinner with. Her and Zack."

Connor nods with a smile. "I'm excited to meet them."

I lock up, and we head to the restaurant.

The place is nice. Italian food is my favorite, and the preliminary bread basket helps break up some of the tension.

Zoe has taken the opportunity to show off the full force of her ability to dress to the nines. Her hair is half up, locks of gold lightly curled and streaming down her back. An off the shoulder pale pink dress ends just above her knees and is accented with vibrant touches of brilliant bubble-gum pink embroidery. The earrings match the necklace, match the bracelet, match the hair clip... she's perfection. Simple as that.

Hard to believe my barbie bestie is also a serial killer, but the thought flashes through my mind when she picks up the butter knife and takes it to her bread, the metal catching the light and winking at me.

Zack arrives last.

He isn't wearing black. Instead, a dark green suit, like ivy at midnight, fits him like a glove. He's left it unbuttoned, the shirt underneath a pale gray and opened a bit more than my date's. With his black hair slicked back, his shoes polished, and his silver cufflinks matching the glint on his lobes, he's what I'd picture Asian Bruce Wayne looking like.

My throat goes dry, and a bit of water dribbles down my chin as I busy myself with avoiding Zoe's calculating eye. Connor stands for each entrance, hand out and chest lightly puffed as he greets my friends. Zoe declines as politely as she is able and, with my advance warning, Connor isn't offended. Zack takes his hand with a firm grip and shakes it.

I watch, waiting for the smartass look when Connor says, "It's so nice to meet Karrie's friends."

But Zack keeps a smile on his face, and his eyes on Connor. "Yeah, Connor. Back at ya. She's said a lot of nice things."

Connor blushes. I do too before catching Zack's wink to Zoe and rolling my eyes. We settle in and my friends do a surprisingly good job of maintaining chill and relaxed conversation. There is no talk of murder, no mention of what happened to my numerous exes, and enough subtly in their sass that Connor doesn't notice or ignores it.

"So," Zoe says as the waiter leaves with our orders, "where did you go to school, CB?"

Connor glances over at me at the same time that Zack nearly chokes on his bread.

"Connor Bradley." I smile and pat his arm.

He does the *ahh* nod and fills Zoe in on an amount of information she absolutely already knows.

My date is sweet. A genuinely nice guy who... ugh, there's that word again. It fits. He's nice. Part of me whispers how boring that is. Another part reminds me that a nice guy isn't liable to be murdered by my best friend.

Another part worries that those deaths Zoe *claims* not to be responsible for mean I really am cursed and that, nice or not, he's destined for a dark end.

My grip tightens momentarily on Connor's arm. He glances over, and I flash a smile. He's fine. Safe. Nice.

My stomach clenches as Zack stands to refill everyone's wine. That suit doesn't make him look nice. It makes my insides melt.

I focus hard on Connor. On what I can have, not what I want. I focus on being a lovely date, getting that goodnight kiss at the end, and heading out just the two of us for ice cream after.

I push Zack, and death, from my mind as we meander with ice creams in hand.

"So, how long have Zack and Zoe been together?" Connor slurps his chocolate cone while I nearly choke on my mint chip.

I cough for half a minute, clear my throat, and break into a laugh that causes Connor's eyes to widen with concern.

"Sorry, sorry." I inhale, calming myself. "In no way, shape, or form are Zack and Zoe together. She's not into anyone that way and Zack... well I don't really know what his type is, but let's just say they wouldn't be compatible."

"Ahh." Connor nods. "That explains it. I just thought they didn't like PDA."

I giggle, licking my ice cream with a suggestive wink. "You know who doesn't mind PDA?"

He laughs and pulls me close, our ice creams outstretched to save us from drips, and plants a kiss on my lips. It's like a scene from a movie.

Heat flares inside me, and I'm sure, at this moment, that I can fall for Connor. I can bring some adventure to his life, and he can bring stability to mine. We can balance each other out.

When we pull apart, he's flush as a tomato.

"So, they're not dating. That explains a few things. But why does she call him Tom?"

I break into another fit of laughter, loop my arm in his, and continue us on our walk.

Chapter Ten

POINTING FINGERS

All I have to say is thank God we didn't invite Captain Bland along on this movie date. It probably wouldn't have been his style anyway. The humor was a little too sharp for him. Not that he isn't smart, but he doesn't catch the wit of most situations. He never laughs at any of my quips, let alone Karrie's. His brow always wrinkles when I crack a joke, and he sort of smiles indulgently at her—once he catches on.

Tom, however, not only picks up on *her* wit, but he actually gets my dry humor. He even joins in. I won't deny that I like him. As much as I have the capacity to like anyone. I'd be absolutely okay with Karrie dating him, which they definitely should do so we don't have to endure Captain Bland. Because even Karrie is clearly bored with him.

But this stupid "curse" she thinks she has—which she would now call *me* and what I call someone else—is cramping everybody's style. I haven't totally worked out who's behind it all and why... yet. But none of us want Tom to end up dead, so we all have to pretend they're not into each other and that Captain Bland is who she wants to be with. To be honest, Tom handles it really well. Which also proves he's just an all-around decent guy.

We say our goodbyes in the parking lot, and I roll my eyes as Tom and Karrie stare just a little too long before getting in their respective vehicles.

I opted to drive, so I'm already behind the wheel when Karrie settles into the passenger seat, sighing heavily. Even in the darkness of the cab at ten o'clock at night, I can see her forcefully shifting gears in her mind.

"You okay?" I ask.

"Fine." She twists in her seat, the sparkle back in her eyes. "Do you mind dropping me at Cap—I mean, Connor's before you head home?"

Ah, so it's going to be one of those nights. Who am I to judge how she's going to blow off steam after the build up of tension that simmers between Tom and her? I sat in between them during the movie, and I could feel their mutual desire to reach for each other. It was part of the reason why I sat there. Neither of them had asked, but it's sort of become our thing. I'm like the sexual tension buffer, which doesn't really bother me except that it's mildly distracting.

Either way, I don't think Captain Bland is going to last long.

"Yep." I turn the key and drive us out of the parking lot toward his place.

The drive is short, and Karrie is texting the whole way there, giggling. That would probably be Tom. Because they do that. We all have a thread going, but she and Tom regularly break off into their own little world.

We pull into the short driveway in front of C.B.'s single-car garage, and I settle in to wait as she hops out and floats up his front steps under the glow of his porchlight. I absolutely will not leave until I know she's safely inside.

She disappears through the front door, and I'm about to pull away when her scream slices through the night air, sending my heart plummeting to my toes.

I leap out of the still-running car as she comes flying back out of the house and down the steps.

"Oh, my God, he's dead," she half-whispers. "He's dead."

I grip her arms and try to catch her wide, glassy-eyed gaze. "Who's dead? Captain Bland?"

Her eyes sharpen on my face, and her hands grip my elbows. "Connor is dead. Zoe, what did you do?!"

I pull my head back. "Why would you assume it was me?"

Her fingers dig into my skin a little. "You are literally the only murderer I know."

If she's able to add that much sarcastic bite to her words, I know she's probably going to be okay, so I urge her to go sit in the car and lock it while I go check on Captain Bland. For all we know, he fell and hit his head and was just unconscious.

But I don't get far—carefully not touching the door—before I come in contact with the copious amount of blood that's pooled on the floor and confirms for me what Karrie had already established: Captain Bland is dead.

There's no way anyone would survive this amount of blood loss, and judging by the pallor of his skin, he's been gone for a couple of hours.

I back up, reaching into my purse for my phone, and glance toward the car. Karrie has the dome light on, and it casts an eerie glow over her face, sharpening her delicate features and giving her a sickly look. But that might also be because she's on the verge of throwing up.

As I answer the questions posed by the 9-1-1 dispatcher, I think through the facts. One, whoever did this had a serious bone to pick with C.B. They'd used a sharp weapon—knife probably—to kill him, hoisting upward and viciously eviscerating him. Two, they were sloppy. Or just didn't care. Based on his placement—right inside the front door—I'm guessing the killer showed up and plunged the implement into his gut upon being greeted, leaving the body sprawled just inside. Three, and this isn't so much a fact as a guess on my part, but this probably has something to do with Karrie very specifically.

The curse—aka the someone who is *not* me—has struck again.

I sit in the car with Karrie while we wait for the authorities to arrive. I grab her hand, feeling how clammy her skin is and check her pale face.

"You going to throw up?"

She shakes her head hard, and I'm suspicious she's not willing to open her mouth in case it's the open invitation for her to upchuck the copious amounts of movie theater popcorn she ingested not an hour before.

"You let me know. I'll hold your hair," I offer, leaning my head back against the seat while we settle in to wait.

She simply squeezes my hand as the faint sound of sirens fills the air. Because they can't take my word as a non-medical person, they send it like they might actually be able to save his life. Have to take precautions.

The ambulance arrives first, followed closely by the police.

Once it's established that he is, in fact, dead, we go around in circles about our connection to him, what we were doing before this, how long we'd known him, where we live, who we were with, why we were here, etc.

And then one of the cops makes the connection between Karrie and another recently discovered dead guy—yep, Trashbag Douchebag strikes again.

They'd already done a second round of questioning with Karrie when his body was found, but now that there's another man whose death is clearly smelling foul—figuratively and literally—Karrie's now much more suspicious than before.

"Miss Dunshire, we're going to need to bring you to the station for further questioning," Cop One says.

She's got her hands wrapped around her elbows, essentially hugging herself, and she stiffens at this turn of events. She shoots me a look that I can't decipher. Or maybe I'm hoping it's not what my initial impression is telling me it is: blame.

Does she still think I did this?

Well, shit.

"We'll figure it out, Kar," I say as they lead her toward the patrol car.

I'm already moving to my car, ready to follow so I can wait for her at the station, whether that's allowed or not.

It's allowed, though grudgingly. It's well past two in the morning when they finally release Karrie. She's pale and hollow-looking with dark circles under her eyes, and her makeup is smudged. Pretty sure she cried at some point.

She lets me put my arm around her and lead her out to the parking lot, both of us shivering when the chill that is deeper in the middle of the night cuts into us.

In the car, she sort of curls into a ball in her seat, and I know she must be exhausted. I am too, but not in the same way. I wasn't held for questioning, though I was absolutely the one they should have had in that interview room.

Guilt wends its way through my gut as I think about the position Karrie's in because I'm partially responsible for it. So I didn't kill Captain Bland. But I did kill Trashbag Douchebag, and both of those deaths are inextricably linked to Karrie. Even the idiotic police would be able to connect that.

If I hadn't done it, she wouldn't be in this position. If I hadn't done it... someone else might have gotten hurt.

We get home in record time since there is little to no traffic, and I shuffle her off to bed.

I doubt she sleeps any better than I do, but I don't bother her. I half expect her to come knock on my door for a middle-of-the-night Psych marathon or something for comfort, but I think she's still upset with me.

When I finally give in and get up, I turn my phone off *do not disturb* and receive a series of texts from TCT expressing his panic about what was going on. I'm not sure when he'd sent each message since they all arrive at once, but I hear the pounding on our door as soon as I walk into the living room.

He practically shoves his way inside when I open the door. Dude has clearly gotten too comfortable with us. I experience my first inkling of dislike. Up to this point, I would likely call him a friend. Like, distantly, but someone I genuinely don't mind. Usually.

But then he quickly takes off his shoes and sets them on the shoe rack neatly, and I'm placated a bit.

"Where's Karrie?" he asks.

I can't place his tone. Concern and something else underneath, and I narrow my eyes at him.

"I'm right here," Karrie says from behind me. She looks terrible, sleepless sunken eyes verifying that she didn't sleep any better than I did.

Tom seems frozen initially, his expression going entirely blank.

Must be the bedhead. Gives him visions of what the morning after with her might look like. Because of course. Dude is so far gone. I roll my eyes.

"What are you doing here, Tom?" I ask as we watch Karrie shuffle toward the kitchen and to the coffee maker, most likely.

He blinks, looking at me and his brain reboots. "I got a call from one of my guys about Captain—I mean, Connor Bradley and that they brought Karrie in."

I stare at him, waiting for some special revelation. "Yeah, we were there, but thanks for recapping for us."

He rushes to the bartop counter that separates the tiny kitchen from the rest of the small living room/dining room combo. "Karrie, this is bad."

She's at the sink, filling the coffee pot with water, and her raccoon eyes dart to his face with a cutting glare that makes him release a soft gasp. "I'm aware, thank you."

His shoulders tighten, his fingers going white against the vinyl countertop. "Did... did you kill him?"

"Are you fucking serious?" Karrie demands, sloshing some of the water in the pot. "If you really think I did, why the hell would you come here?"

He pulls back in the face of her scalding tone, and I fight my smirk, folding my arms across my chest. He's never experienced this side of Karrie. She's bubbly and light and takes things in stride, so people often underestimate her, thinking she's a doormat.

He sputters. "I-I—"

"You, what?" she snaps. "For a smart guy, Zack, you're such a fucking idiot."

He glances at me.

If he's looking for support, he sure isn't going to get it from me. I just stare at him.

He licks his lips, his eyes following Karrie as she stomps out of the kitchen. "I don't *want* to think you're a murderer. But what am I supposed to do with this evidence?"

Her chin juts out as she puts her hands on her hips. "The evidence doesn't *matter* when you've gotten to know me.

Why would I jump in to help you figure out what's going on and then murder someone?"

He swallows. "To throw off suspicion?"

That's a fair guess, I have to admit. It's a clever way to redirect, and it is kind of what I was doing. A smart murderer would do that. So I absolutely see where he's coming from. Just like I can see where she's coming from.

Because, based on her accusatory looks while she continues to argue with Tom, she definitely still thinks I had something to do with Captain Bland's death. She should know by now, though, that I do have standards. I thought I made it clear that I only take out the horrible human beings.

With a sigh, I attempt to tune out the argument as they go back and forth, figuring I'll give them a moment. It's the most impassioned lovers' quarrel I've ever heard, though the subject matter might be a little unorthodox.

I pour myself a cup of coffee because, of course, Karrie still loves me and is a decent human being so she made enough for all of us. I take it straight. Then I head for the front door to give myself something to do while they fight, banking on a morning newspaper (they still give those out, right?) being out there.

The sun is bright against our front door, and I squint against it, my gritty eyes definitely not rested enough for that kind of abuse. Sure enough, there's the paper. I grab it just as a blue sedan rolls by slowly. The driver is looking intently at me, so I salute him with the rolled paper. It's not the first time a man (or woman) has ogled me from a vehicle.

I snap the paper open, not exactly eager to head back inside because their voices are still raised. And lo and behold, what do I find here? An article about Captain Bland's death. How convenient that they give an estimated time of death, which puts it squarely during the previews of our movie. All three of us walked into that theater together, and no one walked out until the end, all as a unit.

I grin and take a deep breath of the crisp air outside. Probably going to wear my lucky sweater today.

Heading back inside, I hum a little tune as I tuck the paper under my arm, savoring the moment until I can dramatically whip it out.

I spot them standing near the kitchen table. Ooh, I can slap it down with flair and draw their eyes. Have it play out like some sort of movie. Yes, I like this plan.

They don't even move as I walk toward them then sort of shove between them. The satisfying *thwack* of the paper on the distressed surface of the table makes Karrie jump, and they both look at me incredulously.

I smile benignly. "They printed an article about Captain Bland's death already."

They both blink at me. Karrie looks like she's about to cry. Actually, so does Tom.

"Guess what?"

More staring.

"Time of death is 7:21pm."

Tom sucks in a sharp breath. "We got to the theater at 7."

My smile grows. "Yep."

His eyes grow wide, and he pivots back to look at my best friend. "Karrie—"

Her hand shoots up, practically right in front of his face. "Save it."

Okay, I was expecting her to let him apologize, but she turns her back to him and walks toward the kitchen, probably for her own coffee.

Tom swallows hard, shifts like he's not sure what to do, then spins on his heel and walks out the front door.

Well, that didn't go quite as well as I'd hoped.

Chapter Eleven

PIVOT

Fuck.

Zack is out the door and I'm... I'm about to cry.

Why do I always cry? Zoe doesn't cry. Zoe is a stoic example of holding one's emotions in tact and not crumpling under the weight of feeling like a bitch.

To be fair, she doesn't have as many emotions and enjoys that fact.

"You know," Zoe says after a long moment of silence following the slam of the door. "You were blaming me for CB's murder not so long ago."

I swallow, guilt pooling in my stomach as a metallic taste coats my tongue. The image of Connor, sliced open like a piece of meat, is still present at the edge of my mind.

Also, I blamed my best friend for murdering the overly nice guy she already told me was fine.

"I'm sorry," I mutter. I pick at the edge of my black nails. The polish is already pretty far gone. I demolished most of it while sitting in a holding room at the police station all night. "I know it wasn't you. And—" I hold up a hand as she opens her mouth— "not just because of the time of death. I'm sure you know plenty about how to fudge shit like that. I know you didn't do it because you said you didn't do it."

She muffles her smile at my compliment. "First, you're right. It's not that hard to put someone on ice. Second, I forgive you. It's a fair reaction. You *do* only know one serial killer."

I give a weak chuckle and grab a tissue for my nose.

"Third." She comes up and rubs her hand up and down my arm. "Tom's reaction was fair too. You knew you were a suspect when you started falling for him."

I jerk back and stare at her, wide eyed and startled.

"What? You thought you were being subtle or something?" she snaps playfully. "It's like sitting between two cats in heat every fucking day."

My jaw drops even as laughter splits through the horror and fear and sadness and frustration. "Okay, well, yeah I guess I overreacted a bit. But also, I know I can't date him."

She raises an eyebrow. "Why not?"

I grimace. "He's got some secret about his past he won't tell me. I'm not going out with a guy who has secrets. Not anymore."

"Oh, that." Zoe waves a nonchalant hand and my eyes go wide again. "Don't worry, it's nothing kill-worthy."

"I—"

"I'm not telling you," she says with a raised eyebrow. "That's his business. But it's not killing puppies or anything."

I click my tongue against my teeth, irritation eating through the absolute zero patience I have left. "Fine. But there's whoever did... *that*... to Connor. I can't..." I swallow. "I can't put Zack in danger like that."

"Maybe not." Zoe nods. "But you do need to clear the air with him. Even if you two can't be together until we figure this out, he's still our friend."

This drops my jaw as far as it goes. A disbelieving grin slides across my lips, and Zoe is the one holding up a hand now. Her horrified expression makes me want to burst into laughter.

"Hang on," she sputters. "I meant your friend. He's *your* friend."

"Nooo." I cackle. "You said *our*. That means you like him too. That means you, Zoe Turner, have two whole friends."

She shakes her head, turning away. "I take it back. Don't go after him. Let him hate us forever."

Her dry tone pulls another laugh from me, even as I reach for my purse and start pulling on my shoes.

"Keep your cell phone on," Zoe calls after me as I open the door. "And text me if anyone seems suspicious."

It says something about how much time Zack and I have spent together in the last couple of months that I have an idea of where he's gone. The drive downtown is short, and I find a spot right by the river. My stride catches some stares—combat boots and black lace tend to do that, but I'm also nearly jogging.

It only takes a minute. Zack is facing away from me, but my stupid heart knows it's him. The way his hands are shoved into his pockets—like he does when trying to work out a problem. The quarter tilt of his head—frustrated. The rumpled hair—he ran his hands through it a fair amount while he was walking.

He turns as I walk up, my footsteps more hesitant than I'd like. His hands leave his pockets, and his head tilts more, confusion on his face.

"What are you—"

"I'm sorry I yelled at you," I interrupt. "And I'm sorry I got so mad about you accusing me. I know how it looks and I..." My face flushes. "I was more hurt than angry, I think."

A smile hooks the corner of his lip. "You seemed pretty angry."

"Yeah." I huff, a smile cracking my lips as well. "You came in and asked me if I killed the guy I was dating. Right after I got released from holding at the cop shop. Also, I haven't slept in, like, thirty hours or something."

He nods, taking a step closer to me. "For the record, *I'm* sorry I came in like that. I couldn't reach you guys, my contact with the police was freaked, and I... I shouldn't have said what I did. I know you'd never kill someone. Connor was a good guy. I know you'd never do that."

My thundering heartbeat slows. There's a flash of guilt in my gut because, though he's right, I do know a lot more than I'll ever be able to tell him.

He's close now, only a foot away and reaching a hand toward me. I take it. His fingers are warm from his pockets. Mine are cold.

"I, uh..." He's the one turning pink now.

I squeeze his fingers and put my other hand on his chest. It's warm, comforting, sturdy as I lean in, resting my forehead on his shoulder for a few seconds. "I really like you, Zack."

He swallows. I smile into his shirt, then lean my head back to meet his eye.

"I've had Zoe since we were kids," I say. "But everyone else has always been surface-level. No matter how hard I try, making real connections never seems to work out. But with you..."

"It's easy," Zack fills in. "Easier than it should be to talk to you, to spend time with you. I've only known you for a couple months, but... I like sitting in silence with you better than I do talking to most people."

My mouth is dry, my usual confidence somehow shredded by his words. His eyes are bright, his mouth so close to mine...

I lean forward, watching his eyes go wide just before mine flutter closed.

He meets me halfway, and the feel of his lips on mine sends a shock through my system. Heat melts my core. His tongue dances across my lips and I open them, the kiss deepening as my arms lock around his neck. His hands go to my waist, pulling me closer and then circling to my lower back until my body is flush with his.

The world fades out of view. Sound diminishes as only Zack's breathing keeps a steady beat. Like a song only we are dancing to.

Somewhere, far from the alcove of romance we've found ourselves in, a car door slams hard enough to break through.

I jerk back, breathing fast, heartbeat slamming against my chest.

Zack's breaths are short, his eyes wide again as he grins at me. He runs a hand through his hair. "I, uh... that was..."

"Yeah." I smile, and then an image slams into my mind. Connor, mangled and bloody on the floor of his townhouse foyer, his eyes still wide, horrified, and scared.

I step back, fear and guilt creasing my brow. Zack makes to move with me, but I put my hand on his chest again, this time to keep him back.

"What's wrong?" he asks, hurt drawing his lips into a thin line.

I shake my head, tears burning again at the edges of my eyes. "Nothing's changed," I whisper.

"What?"

"Nothing's changed," I say again, louder.

He frowns at me.

I shake my head. "The men I date..." I swallow down my nausea. "We can't, Zack. Not until we find who killed Connor and the others. It's not..." I look down, wringing my hands together to avoid the urge to take his again. "It's not safe."

His voice is shaky. "You're right."

I twist my lips to the side, fighting the itching in my nose and tears in my eyes. I take another step back, bringing my arms up and hugging myself as my fingers pick at my sweater.

"We'll find who's doing this, Karrie."

He sounds more sure this time, but it still feels like my heart is cracking. I already got one man killed this month; the thought of finding Zack that way...

"Yeah," I mutter. "I'm going home. I'll see you around, Zack."

Chapter Twelve

BEATING THE ODDS

I still don't get who would be out to get these guys. Like, my reasoning for killing the others makes sense. Absolute trash human beings the world is better off without. But there's nothing about the ones I'm not responsible for that screams "Murder me!"

I can feel in my bones that once we figure out why, we'll have an easier time figuring out who's behind it.

And this definitely has to happen before any connection with me can be made. I was careful, to be sure. But the suspicious disappearances that True Crime Tom has put together are bound to pop up on some detective's radar now that two men have been found dead while actively dating Karrie, and one of them is my handiwork.

She might easily get cleared of suspicion because she often has rock-solid alibis (thanks to my careful planning). But that doesn't mean they wouldn't connect anyone else in her life, and given that I am—ahem—actually responsible for the deaths of a portion of these guys, I'm in serious danger of being found out.

I'd covered my tracks so well, but how the hell was I supposed to know some other—sloppy—serial killer would throw off the groove and put the whole operation in danger? I'm a planner, but there was no way for me to anticipate that pitfall.

The one thing I can be sure of is the connection to Karrie. No way did these other guys just *happen* to date Karrie then die "accidentally" and one brutally via homicide. So if I consider all of their deaths murders, statistically speaking, it would have to be the work of one person.

Sure, Karrie already was beating the odds by having a link to one serial killer. The fact that she's connected to two puts her situation into the astronomical category. Like, winning the lottery odds. Actually, probably more remote than that.

Even with the very large list of men she's dated (and since research shows that men are more likely to commit murder), those odds are so beyond comprehension that it seems ridiculous to even consider it.

So outside of that, it's clear it has to be the same killer because they all died shortly after or while dating Karrie, and every one of them was under suspicious circumstances. No one can convince me the surfer who drowned and the guy whose brakes were faulty aren't fishy. Marcus Kennedy being robbed and beaten to death already screams foul play, but add in the timing, and it can't be ignored.

And this careless asshole is the reason everything I've done to cover my ass is falling apart. But maybe... Maybe he can be the one who gets me out of it.

There's half a dozen men who've disappeared thanks to me, but at least another half-dozen more are the handiwork of this other killer. Who's to say he can't be responsible for more?

Derek and Vincent were killed in two very different ways (thanks to the decade of time between them and my changing methods), which fits the pattern of this other, more chaotic, psycho. Derek and Captain Bland, however, have some similarities. All it would take is a little leading to help someone idiot onto that path of thought. And if I can get everyone on that line of thinking, Karrie (and I) would be in the clear.

So I need to investigate these other deaths and figure out who this blessing in disguise is and clear our names in the process. Two birds. I am nothing if not efficient.

Before I can form another thought, the deadbolt on our front door clicks, and it's flung open. Karrie breezes in, her hair flying wildly around her, chest heaving with emotion.

"We have to investigate the murders and find out who the other killer is."

She speaks so quickly, it takes me a moment to figure out what she even says.

"Good timing," I reply. "I was just thinking the same thing."

Her mouth closes with an audible click as she narrows her eyes at me. "Wait, why do you want to figure it out? You don't have to hide it from me any more."

It's a good (or maybe concerning?) sign that she's taken the little fact that I have killed (and would again, if necessary) people in stride.

"Yeah, but Tom isn't going to give up investigating any time soon." I point a finger in her direction. "Plus, how are you supposed to go back to your prolific dating life if the threat of your love interest of choice dying is almost a certainty?"

Her lip trembles. "Good point."

What neither of us says, and what I am guessing is the reason she's fighting tears, is that she specifically can't be with Tom, which is the biggest tragedy of all since he actually shows promise as long-term relationship material. And I like him enough to accidentally call him my friend when he's not. He's just a dude.

I heave a sigh. "The most unknown and, therefore, dangerous factor at play is that we don't know who is killing these guys or why. Maybe if we could get to the why, we could figure out the who."

Her shoulders droop. "This would be easier if we didn't have to wade through your kill list."

I shrug. "At least with me, you know why and who."

She gives her eyes such a hard roll, it's gotta be painful. "Yeah, and now I can be sure to avoid anyone you might deem a target."

"I appreciate that. If you're more judicious, I don't have to be so calculating. And my dry cleaning bill will go down."

My eyes track her as she moves to the couch and flings herself down with a huff.

She grimaces, tilting her head and scratching behind her ear. "It feels a little wrong to talk so casually about your... extracurricular activities."

It has never felt quite so taboo to me, but neither have a lot of things that society categorizes as off-limits. "And yet we discuss your 'extracurriculars' in detail and with great enthusiasm."

She pouts again. "At least my extracurriculars are legal."

"But no less disgusting." I shrug. "Mine help society at large, so I fail to see the real problem."

Karrie shoots ramrod straight and gives me an exasperated look. "The real problem is that it's illegal, Zoe."

The corner of my mouth quirks. "So is rolling through a red."

She makes a noise somewhere between a snort and a growl, and probably not just because that was a blatant jab at her. "Not the same thing."

I fold my arms and sit back, smug. "Nope, but if you're going for illegal as the major objection, we're sticking with that track."

She narrows her eyes at me. "What's that supposed to mean?"

"It means that you don't actually think what I've done is wrong if you went for the legality angle instead of the moral one—which is that I've literally killed human beings."

Her mouth opens and shuts like a fish on land a few times. Then she shakes out her hair and waves her hands. "Let's get back to the point."

"Which is?" I hide my grin, loving that she still refuses to deny it.

"Why you feel the need to investigate what's really going on."

I snort. "Besides the fact that whoever took these other dudes out is sloppy and, therefore, sullies my meticulous efforts and deserves to go down?"

Karrie throws her hands into the air. "Zoe!"

"It's a legitimate reason, Karrie."

She speaks through her teeth: "Besides that."

Okay, admittedly I'm worried about my actual motive looking bad. I mean, Karrie's my best friend, and the fact that she hasn't turned me in since finding out I'm a serial killer tells me her threshold for moral boundaries is alarmingly high. And yet this seems to push things just a little far on the scale.

Karrie's exasperation melts, her eyes going softer as she takes in my face and the obvious hesitation I'm communicating via body language. "Zoe, for real."

I take a breath and smooth out my expression, projecting a calm I don't feel. "I am thinking I can pin all of my murders on this guy."

She sucks in a sharp breath, and I feel it like a stab between my ribs. Turns out, I'm not as untouched by the approval of others as I always believed. There's hope for my dark, shriveled heart after all.

But, ugh, what an awful feeling. I've always known Karrie's opinion was pretty much the only one that ever mattered to me, though only to a certain extent. And I've never felt remorse for what I've done in the name of protecting her. But this is a whole new level of vulnerability I didn't expect. Because this affects what comes next, not what has already happened.

Karrie takes several more minutes to answer, and I can see the wheels turning in her mind. Her fingers tap along her thigh very lightly. Is she planning a way to run screaming without drawing my serial killer wrath (as if I would *ever* do anything to hurt her)? Or maybe she's trying to find a way to tap out without being rude.

"I think that's a good idea," she finally says, just as my skin begins to itch with worry and anxiety.

"You do?"

Her brows pull together, her head tilting slightly. She can probably hear the uncertainty in my tone, a rare occurrence for me. "Zoe, I might not approve of your methods for protecting me, but I really appreciate the danger you put yourself in to do it." She looks down at her hands. "No one's ever done anything like that for me."

"Well, most people draw the line at murder, understandably. It's a lot of work."

She laughs, but it sounds like she was about to cry. "I just mean the lengths you're willing to go... for me."

I reach out to squeeze her hand. "You're absolutely worth murdering for, Kar. I'd do it all again in a heartbeat."

She sniffles and looks at me. "That's why I'll help you pin it on this other guy. I owe you that much."

My heart swells, and it's almost painful. I would absolutely hate the feeling if it weren't for the fact that it's simply because it's Karrie. Someone totally worth feeling miserable for—my best friend, my sister, my family.

"I really appreciate your willingness to help me. But I also think it's worth making this douche suffer since he's taken out every decent guy you've ever dated."

She gets really quiet as she considers that. She might not have noticed that pattern, but I certainly did. Because, obviously, I would have gotten to them first if they'd sucked.

Given the stakes and what we have to accomplish, I know this has to stay under wraps, though.

"Anyway," I say in a measured tone. "We can't let True Crime Tom help us."

Karrie flinches at his name, and it confirms my suspicion that the reason she'd come in with emotional guns blazing was because of the whole Tom thing.

"Obviously, he can't know I'm responsible for some of these guys. But it sucks because he's actually really good at this investigating stuff."

Karrie gasps theatrically. "Zoe Leanne Turner, did you just compliment another human being?"

I curl my lip. "I can admit that he's been helpful."

She gives me a smug grin, then it falls a little. "Maybe we can still scooby with him, but keep the side investigation a secret? And he mentioned he has a contact in the police department."

I tip my head to the side, considering. "Yeah, it's a good friend of his from high school."

Karrie scoffs. "Of course you know that."

I shrug. "Just because I like him doesn't mean I didn't dive deep on him."

"That's right." She scoots to the edge of the couch. "Are you going to tell me what his secret is now?"

I stiffen. Oops. "Uhhhhh…"

Both of her hands wrap around my forearm. "You have to tell me!"

I laugh. "I don't, actually."

"Zoe!" she whines. "I told you it's nothing worth killing over." I pat her hand and stand up, heading for the kitchen for a snack.

She huffs in frustration, flinging herself back against the couch cushions. "You're the worst," she mutters.

"Anyway," I continue as I walk. "I like your idea of maybe using some TCT resources without totally bringing him in."

"How are we supposed to do that?" she asks the ceiling.

"His computer." I take a bite of my apple, thoughtful. "You could distract him while I dig on his laptop at our next group scooby time."

"How do I distract him?" she wails, and I seriously wonder if she's joking.

I poke my head out of the kitchen to level a look her way. "Karrie, are you for real?" I ask dryly.

She shifts to meet my eye, genuinely unsure. Like she isn't the most gorgeous thing to walk the earth. Which, I guess, is nice. She has some level of humility. Maybe because it's Tom and not just some rando at the club.

"Wear that shirt and your ass pants. Problem solved."

"That's not enough."

The way I've seen Tom's eyes follow her through the room whenever we're all together begs to differ. The man is so far gone for Karrie, it's ridiculous. And it solidifies my resolve in figuring this whole thing out, just so I can stop wading through the sexual tension that continues to build between them.

"Lure him outside. All I need is, like, ten minutes."
She pouts.
"You have my permission to kiss him if necessary."
Karrie groans. "I did kiss him. And it was amazing."
I make a face. "Then kiss him again."

"That might just kill me."

Or him. But I don't say that out loud because she would probably take it wrong. But I chuckle to myself.

I hold up my hands and walk back out toward her. "Let's just see what we can work out. When is the next scooby-do party?"

Her sigh is like a slow leak, long and drawn-out. "I'll see what I can set up for next week. Right now, I just need some sleep."

"That's fair. We definitely need you on your A-game."

Karrie snorts and rolls her eyes, heading for her room. While she sleeps, I decide to get going on this side investigation.

CHAPTER THIRTEEN

LONG-PAST

I thought scooby-dooing with Zack was difficult before, but ever since our kiss, things have been... awkward.

It doesn't help that Zoe and I can't tell him about our side investigation. She's right though, as usual, if we can pin her murders on whoever-the-fuck is actively destroying every good man I've ever dated, we'll both be safer.

Not to mention she can probably hang up her knives after that. I mean, now that she's given Zack the all-clear, I know she won't kill him. If we are able to date, and it doesn't work out, I'll just make sure she vets everyone I go out with for the rest of my life.

Easy-peasy.

Between now and then, however, I have to ignore the way Zack's eyes linger on me. I have to concentrate on not staring at him the same way. I have to pretend I don't feel the heat when our fingers brush, when he leans around me to grab a file in the tight, clean studio.

I have to ignore Zoe's pointed looks, raised eyebrows, and humorously pursed lips.

She and I climb the steps to Zack's place, sushi in a plastic bag, iced coffee in a cardboard holder. She's got her notebook, filled with scribblings I can barely read. Not because they're untidy, but because she has a coded way of taking notes that I don't quite remember from high school.

Even though we've jumped headlong into this side quest of investigating my other personal serial killer, we haven't gotten much. Someone from my past is responsible. Has to be. The problem with that theory is that the murderous men who might have had a hand in all this are *already dead*, thanks to Zoe. Which leaves us disturbingly lacking in suspects.

Still, there have to be clues somewhere. As Zoe has said a hundred times in the week since Connor was killed, this guy is sloppy.

"Finally," Zack says as a greeting when he opens the door. "I'm starving."

He takes the sushi from my hands and hurries to the table. Zoe nudges my back and I step forward, gritting my teeth against the urge to leave. Instead, I sit across from Zack and pull my own fuzzy black notebook from my petite cheetah print backpack.

Zoe settles in next to me, giving a nod of approval at the cleanliness of Zack's space. The faint scent of lemon clorox lingers in the air. He confessed to me over a month ago that he bought three jumbo packs of wipe dispensers to make sure he doesn't run out.

"All righty, Tom. What've you got?"

Zack glances up with his mouth full of shrimp tempura. He uses his chopsticks to gesture at the bulletin board on the wall. The one strewn with red yarn, pushpins holding it to pictures, maps, crossed out post-it notes with old theories and ideas.

There are two pictures pinned to the front: Derek and Connor. My stomach churns at Connor's innocent smile. Not many people take a good driver's license photo, but his isn't bad.

"Two men." Zack swallows down a large bite and continues, "Killed with a similar weapon. A blade. So far we don't have much in the way of connections between murders and missing people, but this is something new. Whoever is doing this is getting sloppy."

"So far there hasn't been anything consistent between the deaths," Zoe adds. "Why would the killer change things now?"

I don't look at her, keeping my gaze on the pictures on the board. Still, I'm impressed with how even her tone is. She straight up stabbed Derek and is acting like she has no idea who could possibly be responsible.

"Maybe something triggered him to attack?" Zack suggests. For all his talk of being hungry, he pushes his tray of sushi away and crosses to the bulletin board, hands on his hips and a thoughtful frown on his lips.

I heave a sigh. "Something besides me dating them, you mean."

Zack physically cringes.

"Well, duh." Zoe scoffs, continuing her sassy not-the-killer cover. "You've been with plenty of people without them getting killed."

I glare at her while Zack's back is turned.

She shrugs, and I know she's actually trying to be helpful. "Seriously. Trent wasn't murdered. You went on a date with him between Derek and Connor. There was something else that triggered this wacko to slaughter him."

I wince. "Them."

"Right." Zoe picks up a piece of sushi with her chopsticks, unbothered by the potential slip up. "Them."

Zack returns to his seat and pulls a bowl of wasabi closer to him. "So death by stabbing checks off one box—something that ties them together. Then there's some missing piece about Karrie's relationships with them—another tie, but we don't know what it is."

"Yep." Zoe nods and eats a piece of ginger, sucking on it before chewing it up.

I shake my head at the nonchalance of the two of them. Two months ago, this whole conversation would have made me vomit. However, there's sushi to eat, and my life isn't getting any less gross anytime soon. I dig in as Zack and Zoe continue chatting. When the food is finished, Zack returns to his computer and boots it back up.

"Couple more things," Zack says.

Zoe follows him. "Whatcha got, True Crime Tom?"

I stack the empty sushi cartons and put them in the bag, setting it by the door before heading over.

"Wait," Zack says, pausing while sifting through files on his screen. "That's where the 'Tom' comes from?"

"Yep," Zoe replies with zero inflection in her voice.

I settle onto a stool beside Zack, a smile twisting my lips at the expression on Zack's face.

"That's..." he groans. "That's an amazing name for a podcast. Damn it."

Zoe nods. "Pity you've already built a brand around Armchair Detective."

I snort.

Zack shakes his head, heaves a sigh, and returns his focus to the computer. "Right. Moving on from regrettable life choices... Here's what I've got."

A series of pictures comes onto the screen. They appear to be street camera shots, all of pieces of a large blue sedan. None show the driver.

Zoe's eyes narrow, and I recognize the look of concentration on her face. She's connecting dots.

"These were taken all over the city, but most are from around the downtown area." Zack clicks the mouse a few times, scrolling through more images, pulling up a map, and continuing to talk.

Most of what he says is lost on me because Zoe has shifted from concentration to miming.

She stares at me, points at Zack behind his back, and then points to the door. I shake my head. Now is not the time, he's literally still speaking.

She jerks her head at the computer. Zack still chatters away, the excitement over his developments clear in his tone. Okay, she wants access to his stuff while the computer is on.

I shake my head, clenching my jaw with pursed lips and trying to silently explain there is no good excuse to get him away. Not to mention the awkwardness that has been plaguing us since Connor's death.

Zoe gives me an exasperated eye roll and begins making kissy faces, pointing from me to Zack and back again.

"So, what do you think?" Zack turns just as Zoe's face returns to her normal smooth expression.

"Interesting." Zoe nods. "Good to have a vehicle to keep an eye out for. I don't notice much of a pattern on the map though."

My eye twitches.

How the hell did she catch everything he said?

Zack turns back to the computer and Zoe gives me her *I'm serious, just fucking do it* look.

I roll my eyes.

"Hey, Zack." My voice sounds robotic.

He glances up at me, those creamy brown eyes wide and interested. Dammit.

"Ice cream? To wash down the sushi?"

Zoe crinkles her nose, so does Zack. Not my best excuse for something, but he stands up anyway.

"Sure. Zoe?"

"Grab me a strawberry." She sounds distracted and has moved back to the bulletin board with what appears to be deep concentration.

Zack clicks off his monitor, stands, and gestures for me to lead the way. I do, stooping to grab the garbage before hurrying down the stairs.

"How are you holding up?" Zack asks after we dump the garbage into a bin on the street and start the two block walk to the ice cream place.

I pick at the edges of my long lace sleeves and let the question sit for a moment. He—unlike any other man I've met—gives me a full minute of contemplation to answer. "I'm... not good."

He runs a hand through his hair and glances at me. "Yeah, that was maybe a dumb question."

"No, I'm glad you asked."

"You know none of this is on you, right?"

I clench my jaw, rubbing a hand up and down my arm as a chilly breeze blows down the street. "I'm not sure how true that is, but thanks."

Zack shakes his head and digs his hands into his front pockets. The man sure does look good in a pair of jeans.

"I think we're close, Karrie. There's some connection. Some missing piece that will click into place, and then we'll find this guy and then—"

He falters, face flushing as we come to a stop in front of the ice cream shop. The sight of his cheeks darkening sends heat to my core.

"And then I can live my life without worrying that I'm getting people brutally murdered?" I give half a laugh and a weak smile to emphasize the fact that I'm joking. Even though it's not exactly a joke.

"Yeah, that."

An hour later, Zoe and I climb into the car and head back home. We've barely pulled away from the curb when she flips open her notebook and starts running through the information she's put together.

"Okay. Rando from your past is killing guys."

"But not all the guys," I add.

She nods. "Just the non-toxic ones, it seems."

"Which means that, combined with you, just about every guy I've been on more than a few dates with has ended up missing."

"Exactly. Well, missing or dead, since clearly this guy isn't great at hiding bodies."

I give a little shake of my head at her laissez-faire tone. "Is part of you wanting to find him so you can give him a lesson in proper murder etiquette?"

"If you're gonna do something, do it right."

I open my mouth, close it again, and return my attention to the road. A moment passes while she flips pages and cuts dashes across her papers in bright pink highlighter.

Connor and I were together for a couple weeks, but I doubt even he would say we were getting *serious*. I tap the steering wheel, inhaling a lungful of air that doesn't quite fill my lungs. The other men we assume this asshole is responsible for were serious. As serious as I've gotten, anyway.

Zoe is muttering. I focus up.

"What?"

"I was just saying that I've seen the car before."

My hands jerk at the wheel. "*What?*"

"Yeah, out front of the apartment one time, and then downtown when we've gone out. I've seen it here and there, but I didn't put it together until looking at Tom's computer. I'm sure you've seen it too."

I strain my mind. There are too many things here, too many details to focus on. Zoe is good at details. I'm good at the big picture. She could tell you the date of every battle in the Civil War. I can tell you why each battle mattered.

Still, the image flickers in my mind. I *have* seen it before. The vivid memory of biceps and the scent of blueberries strikes me.

"Yeah, around the smoothie shop. But I don't remember the last time I saw it. I think it was there when I met Trent."

Zoe clicks her tongue. "So Stalker–"

"Is that the name we're going with?"

A shrug. "Until I think of something better. Stalker probably saw you meet Unsmooth Smoothie Guy."

"But didn't kill him."

She purses her lips. "Unfortunately."

My eyes go wide, and I gape at her.

"Joking! That was a joke."

I heave a sigh as I pull the car into our designated parking spot. "You can't make those jokes anymore, Zoe. Cuz they're not actually jokes most of the time."

She climbs out of the car and winks. "True, but now you get all the hilarious thoughts I've been holding in to protect you."

I follow her up the steps, clicking the lock on my keys and feeling slightly comforted by the little beep behind me.

We go in, take off our shoes, and both tap the bracelet hanging on the wall.

The bracelet.

I stare at Zoe, cogs clicking into place as she strides across the floor in her white socks, doing a twirl when she reaches the hall.

"It's you."

She turns back and cocks her head at me.

I move forward in something of a daze, resting my butt on the back of the couch and folding my arms. "It's you, Zoe."

She does the *more please* gesture.

"What happens when I get serious with a guy? When, on the rare day I find someone I actually like who likes me back and isn't blacklisted by your sleuthing skills?"

She thinks it over, striding back to me with a furrow in her brow. "Me?"

"Yeah. Think about it." I hold up a finger. "You met Logan on my birthday. We had that whole beach party he threw together. It was the first time you met him. We parted ways a week after that, and then I never heard from him again." I put up another finger. "Marcus was at Thanksgiving dinner at your parents'. It was the first time you met him. And David–"

"The phone call," Zoe murmurs, her fingers lightly hovering over her lips, bright eyes wide.

"Exactly."

It was a weeklong extravaganza of wedding related activities. David and I had half a dozen Hallmark movie moments, sneaking away from rehearsal dinners, finding gazebos in the rain, solving the bridal bouquet problem together and, in the bride's words, saving the wedding. It was romantic, it was hot, and at the end of the week, once the wedding was over and the couple had jetted off on their honeymoon, I called Zoe.

David lived across the country. Zoe and I had just decided to get another fresh start somewhere, and I suggested his city.

But then I stopped hearing from him. No text, no calls, no emails. Ghosted.

We decided on a different adventure, once I stopped crying.

"He knows *me*." Zoe's voice has an underlying current of horror. Not terror, like a normal person would feel. More what I'd expect her to sound like if someone marched through the house with sewer worker's boots on.

I nod. "He knows *us*. You're my family, Zoe. A guy meeting you is basically bringing him home to meet the parents. Whoever this psycho is... he knows how important you are to me."

"And bringing Connor to dinner—"

"Was enough to make Stalker think I loved him."

Zoe exhales.

My stomach is in knots, back tense, jaw aching from how hard I've been clenching my teeth. The windows suddenly seem too wide. The door is locked, but I stare at the deadbolt for a long few seconds just to be sure.

Zoe crosses the room and pulls the curtains closed.

I swallow hard. "We need to look further back."

She nods, moving down the hallway to close the curtains in our rooms as well. I follow her, arms still tight over my chest.

When she's done, she returns to stand in front of me. Her blue eyes are just above mine, that tall physique only adding to her Barbie-like frame. There is anger in those eyes right now. More, possibly, than I've seen since the night I left Vincent.

"We're going to fix this, Kar."

I nod. "Together, right?"

My heart pounds in my chest. The fear that Zoe is going to run off and try to solve this problem alone–like she has every other problem-with-a-penis in my life–clutches my heart. I don't want her doing this alone. I don't want her to have to save me, again.

She hesitates a split second before nodding. Her hands go to my shoulders and she pulls me into a hug. "Together. Promise."

Chapter Fourteen

SLOPPY

Karrie and Tom not being able to date has seriously sucked all the fun out of movie nights. Neither of them pay attention to the screen because they're hyper aware of each other, and all their sneaky glances and *Ooh, sorry* every time they accidentally touch distracts *me* from what's happening.

But I say nothing, despite being annoyed as hell. It's probably my fault for not sitting between them like I usually do, but I thought they could be adults about this.

Once the movie ends, Karrie walks Tom slowly to the door, doing her languid, flirty walk (she's wearing The Pants again. Will she never learn?), and laughing at whatever he's saying. I've tuned them out already because he'll linger for a while as he usually does.

I go to the kitchen to double-check the dishes we'd cleaned from dinner. TCT helped, and even though he's picked up on my OCD cleanliness, he hasn't quite mastered the level of clean I prefer for dishes.

"I was going to do that," Karrie says from behind me.

"I don't mind," I reply quickly.

She ignores me and joins in on re-scrubbing the pans TCT used to make us one of his mother's Malaysian recipes. An uncharacteristic silence falls over us. For clarity-sake, it's uncharacteristic of her, not me.

I glance over, noting that her lips are pressed into a tight line, and I know instantly that something is bothering her. And I doubt it's only the frustration of not being able to pursue something with Tom.

"Okay, you going to spit it out, or do I have to torture it out of you?"

She doesn't even crack a smile, but she also doesn't look horrified. "That's not funny, Zoe."

I lift a shoulder. "It kind of is." She still doesn't smile. "Okay. What's bothering you? And please don't say it's not getting into Tom's pants."

She groans and throws the steel wool scrubber into the sink, burying her face in her hands. "No! It's the fact that I want to."

I *had* thought this wasn't the factor underlying her upset, but perhaps I read the situation wrong. Not that it's not worth feeling disappointed about (from her perspective), but I'd thought it would be something a little more serious.

"It's not bad to be attracted to someone," I say, finishing my scrubbing and rinsing the pan off. "I imagine it's kind of nice—if they like you too."

Her mouth quirks for a second. Then she sucks in a deep breath and noisily lets it out for several seconds. "Do you think there's something wrong with me?"

I scoff. "No. I mean, aside from your ad nauseum discussed terrible taste in men. But no one's perfect."

She nibbles her lip, and it might not be my imagination that her chin trembles a little.

I fold my arms and lean my hip against the counter. "Karrie, what is it, really?"

"Connor died, like, two weeks ago."

I am not sure where she's going with this, so I maintain my neutral expression. "He did," I confirm.

"And I haven't stopped thinking about Tom—er, Zack since."

My tongue clicks. "Karrie, you were thinking about him *before* Captain Bland died."

A growly groan rumbles out of her as she stomps out of the kitchen. "That's what I mean! Why can't I like nice guys?"

My brows pull together as I follow her into the living room. "Tom's a nice guy."

She pauses for a second, tipping her head to acknowledge that. "Yeah, but the *reason* I wasn't dating him was because he has a secret, and I couldn't let you kill him!"

I can't help a little laugh. "It's not a secret worth killing over," I remind her.

She throws her hands into the air. "I wish I'd known that before dating Captain Bland!" Then she shakes her head, flopping into my desk chair. "I mean, Connor."

That is a bit of a tragedy. She spent time with the most boring guy on the planet, thinking she was protecting Tom, only to put Captain Bland into danger. Not that she could have known what would happen, but still.

"I mean, look at this!" She spins to wake up my computer, bringing up her social media accounts. She clicks onto pictures and scrolls through the numerous snapshots of the various men she's dated.

Face after face. There's no denying that Karrie has a type. Chiseled body, handsome face, charming smile. And strangely, the clean-cut, polo or button-down wearing type, which seems quite at odds with her glam-goth style.

"Marcus was a nice guy," I say, jabbing a finger toward his picture on the screen.

"But that proves my point. I didn't *really* like Marcus." She keeps scrolling.

I gesture again at the screen. "You liked Surf Bro. He was a nice guy."

Her shoulders droop. "And he's dead."

"At least that one wasn't me."

She gives me a dark look.

Not that I cared much for Surf Bro. He was literally too much of a bro for my taste, but he treated Karrie well. If that had been long-term, I would have had to keep my distance because he annoyed the shit out of me. But Sloppy Stalker made that a moot point anyway.

As Karrie continues scrolling, I genuinely start to wonder why she takes so many pictures, and especially of herself with these one-hit-wonders. Sure, some of them are the ones I took out, and some of them are the handiwork of her stalker. But there are also these really terrible dudes. And there are a lot of them.

We even make it back to the high school days when she'd actually dabbled with goth/emo guys, though they were short-lived. She discovered pretty quickly that, despite her personal style, she was not into goth boys. And then she started dating Vincent, her first and only long-term relationship.

"This is so depressing to look through," she says.

I sigh heavily, unhappy that she's in one of these dark places. She gets to this point on occasion, when society makes her feel broken. It doesn't help that her parents often made her question her worth throughout her life. They were real pieces of work.

The desire to reassure her is strong. "There's nothing wrong with enjoying men, Karrie."

She's looking at the computer screen as she scrolls much less manically, but she doesn't appear to be taking in the images. "I just feel bad that Connor is dead, and I already moved on."

"You were never in it with him. And that's okay. Sure, he was good on paper—just like Marcus. But that doesn't mean you have to like him or settle for him. And that's really what it is: settling."

Her mouth twists to the side, and she finally looks at me again.

My smile is genuine and, hopefully, conveys how truly I believe this. Because, yes, she's dated some real duds. But that's mostly because she likes a pretty face and a nice bod. Most of them aren't guys she'd keep around long-term anyway. But there were some decent guys in the mix. They're in the pictures she has pulled up, and I'm about to point them out to her when my eyes land on one very deep throwback.

My mouth drops open slightly. "I know that guy."

She turns back to look, then snorts. "Of course you do. You don't forget a first date. Blech."

I shake my head, eyes glued to the image. His face is round with youth, his hair long, dark and covering one eye, but that's not what triggers my memory.

"No, I've seen him recently."

"What?"

Something in her tone, and the puzzle piece that slides into place in my mind sends ice spreading through my stomach. I realize it's her fear that's triggered it. Like she already knows where this is going.

"He's been around," I say quietly, my mouth a little dry.

Her wide eyes shift to me. "What do you mean 'around?'"

"It didn't click before. He just seemed like a local who must live nearby since he frequents a lot of the places we do. But now that I'm looking at this old picture..." I tap the screen, his scrawny arm thrown around Karrie's shoulders. I can see her lack of interest even in her body language in the picture. "He's from back home. From our past."

She shoots out of the chair like she's seen a spider. "You think he's my stalker?"

I set my jaw. "There's one way to find out."

I sit in the dark cab of my car, eyes glued to Karrie sitting in the smoothie shop. Her leg shakes like mad, making the table wobble, and she keeps conspicuously glancing toward the door.

It's our little stake-out mission to see if my suspicions are correct. After Karrie finished her shift at the boutique, I had her go to the smoothie shop she frequents. If we can confirm who our Sloppy Stalker is, then we have a thread to follow and a plan to lay out.

"Stop wiggling," I warn, and she flinches at my voice in her bluetooth earbud. "You're going to give yourself away."

"I am so freaked out right now."

Craning my neck, I check for any sign of Reggie Stevens. I know he's gotta be here, would put money on him scoping the place out.

After my little discovery, I did what I do best and found out just how long dear, old Reginald has been keeping track of Karrie. Who knew a high school crush could turn so deadly?

I tracked his addresses and jobs, finding a trail that was alarmingly paralleled with ours. Karrie basically followed me to college out of state (she didn't attend, but she was my roommate for the four years of undergrad). And guess who followed Karrie. That's right. Reginald Stevens III.

As soon as I made the connections, finding that he'd started a new job right around the time we moved here, I knew he was our man.

"Do you see him?" Karrie's voice is tight with apprehension, and it sends my wandering mind into high alert, and I check again.

"Nothing so far. It's only been ten minutes. He'll show."

I suspect he's watching her to see if she lures any other man candy in or if he has a shot at getting her attention. Based on the physical changes he's made over the years, it's clear he's paid enough attention to have picked up on what Karrie tends to go for.

The problem is, he hasn't quite nailed it. Not enough to pop up on her radar, at least. His mistake, however, was in approaching me. Karrie might not remember a face to the last nano-detail, but I have a mind for minutiae.

His general facial structure and build has never changed, even if he'd apparently spent the last fifteen years building muscle and had gotten a decent hair cut.

I hear Karrie's suppressed gasp over the speaker phone and zero in on the door Sloppy Stalker has just walked through. He glances at her, his hands flexing, but he goes for the counter to order.

His body language has changed since the last time I saw him. Tension is obvious in every fiber of his being, something I can practically feel, even from here. It might be the reason he was so sloppy with C.B. Especially considering he's done all this work to try to get Karrie to notice him, and she's still passing him up for other guys.

"I remember him," she breathes into the phone, keeping her gaze down, like she's reading emails on it or something. "He was at the club that first night when I made you come out, wasn't he?"

"Yes." I speak quietly too, though it doesn't really matter. He can't hear me. "He wanted me to give you his number."

"He asked me to dance, but I was already vibing with someone else."

Sloppy moves to a table near-ish to Karrie's, his expression hard. I don't like the way he's moving or looking at her.

"Don't look up," I tell her. "Talk to me normally so he knows you're on the phone with someone."

"Why? Is there something wrong?" she asks in a normal volume, and I'm impressed that she doesn't sound as freaked out as she did before he walked in.

"I think he's frustrated. I have no doubt that's why Captain Bland's death was so gruesome."

"What's the plan?" Only the slightest thread of tension leaks into her tone, recognizable to me because of how well I know her.

Sloppy hasn't moved, but I can tell he's paying very close attention to her.

Warning bells go off in my head, and I want her out of his line of sight. "I think you should head home."

She straightens, glancing too obviously out the window to where she knows my car is.

"Make a comment about me feeling sick, so he doesn't get suspicious. Especially when you get home and I'm not out in the living room."

"Um, well, I'm sorry you're not feeling well. Do you want me to get you anything before I come home?" she asks, standing and gathering her purse and her half-full smoothie cup. "Okay, well, just head to bed. I'll clean up dinner."

"Nice," I whisper, my grin obvious in my voice. She genuinely sounded convincing. "Stay on with me, but pretend to hang up."

She follows my instructions, working very hard not to look at Sloppy as she passes, though he's openly watching her now.

I start my car but wait until she gets into her own. Since I work from home and I rarely go anywhere, we almost always opt to take her car since she prefers to drive anyway. The fact works heavily in our favor. I'm banking on the fact that he won't recognize my vehicle.

"He's going to follow you, I'm sure," I say, pulling away from the curb only once she has. "When you get home, just go inside and watch TV for a bit. I want to see what he does." I pause as I switch lanes, though it's really because I don't want to tell her the next part. She's going to argue with me, guaranteed. "After a while, turn it off and go to bed. I'm going to see if he leads me back to wherever he lives."

"Zoe!"

"It's the best chance we have. I won't go in." *I don't think.* I look over at my sleek black briefcase—technically an attache—slightly larger with plenty of cushioning for my collection of knives.

"Fine," she grumbles. "Are we hanging up now?"

A chill dances along my skin. "Not until you're in the apartment, the door is locked, and I have eyes on Sloppy Stalker."

I swear I hear her gulp on the other end.

We make it home pretty quickly given that the smoothie shop isn't far. I park along the side of the building where I can see in a window, but I'm not in front of our unit, so I'm able to see her when she goes in the front door, habitually taps the bracelet, and takes off her combat boots.

"It's creepy coming home without you here," she says, rubbing her hands over her arms.

My mouth flattens into a line. "I'm here, Kar. Just not inside for once."

She putters around the kitchen for a while, then settles in to watch TV, her grip on the remote entirely too tight to be considered relaxed.

And then I see the shadow of a man shifting along the side of the building, and my lungs trap my oxygen for a moment.

"I've got eyes," I whisper. "I'm hanging up but keep your phone close."

"Okay," she squeaks.

How Sloppy Stalker manages to stand outside our apartment in complete stillness for so long, I have no idea. Literal psycho right there. And the longer he stands and watches, the more my blood boils when I realize how often he must do this.

Karrie watches TV for close to an hour before she finally shuts it off and heads to her room. It's not a stretch that she's going to bed fairly early. She might be a party girl on the weekends, but if she isn't out, she's typically tucked in by ten.

I wait for Sloppy to move on, but he hangs around for a little longer. Maybe waiting for one last glimpse of his obsession.

Finally, the man-shaped shadow shifts, slinking back toward the parking lot that lines the front of our apartment.

He doesn't try to be sneaky once under the glow of the lights out there, and it's easy for me to pull out of my spot and start to follow at a distance with my headlights off.

I might have super good cyber investigative skills, but I have not given enough credit where it's due. Tailing someone in a car is hard. Especially at night and when the traffic is pretty light.

It's a bit of a cat stalking a mouse situation. Can't let on that I'm there, but I have to keep track of him at all times. I think I lose him twice, but I catch back up, my hands twisting on the steering wheel with the intensity of my almost-panic.

He doesn't live far, I find. Pulling into the parking lot of a similarly styled apartment complex, he leads me around to a unit in the back. His place is on the second floor.

My phone vibrates beside me, and I answer without looking at who it is because Karrie's the only person who ever calls me, especially this late. My parents know to text first.

"I'm right outside his place," I say.

"Why do you sound so angry?"

"I can take care of this right now," I offer, my eyes sliding to my knives again.

"No! One, you said we could do this together. And two, we have to plan and be smart. You don't want to be sloppy like him, going in guns blazing."

"I don't use guns."

"Zoe."

Because she has a really solid point, I grudgingly mutter, "Fine."

"Get back here so we can figure out how to take him out."

"Why, Karrie, I do believe that is called premeditated murder."

"Shut up."

I might be grinning as I hang up and start to head home, but the heat of anger continues to simmer through my blood, and I know this guy's days are numbered.

Chapter Fifteen

MURDER BOARD

I'm waiting at the door when Zoe gets home, still flushed with fury, her hands clenched as though she's holding a blade, ready to shove it between Reggie's ribs. She barely looks at me, her focus on the bracelet on the wall as she unzips her heeled boots and sets them neatly on the shoe rack.

It's almost a full minute before she speaks. "Vincent was to protect you."

I blink and step forward, putting a hand on Zoe's arm. "I know."

"He was getting a gun. He was coming back for you. I couldn't let that happen, Kar."

I swallow. "I know, Zoe. It took a minute, but I get it. I'm not... I'm not mad."

Zoe turns to me, her eyes blazing with a look I rarely see. "I am. Sloppy Stalker has been following us for *years*. He's killed the only nice guys you've ever shown an interest in. He's been *watching you*. For *years*."

It clicks in that moment, in the pain in her voice and the tears in her eyes. "You think you should have seen it."

She grits her teeth and looks down.

"Zoe." I step closer, rubbing her arm and ducking to catch her line of sight. "You've kept me safe all our lives. This isn't on you. This is on him. And we're going to take care of it."

The first tear I've seen since we were children rolls down her cheek. She nods. "Tomorrow morning."

"Tomorrow morning," I confirm with a voice that's steadier than I feel. "We pin everything on this asshole, you're free as a bird, and—" I smirk so she catches the joke— "as a thank-you gift, we can stay home for a whole month. Apart from work."

Zoe huffs out a chuckle.

"Sleepover night?"

Zoe steps away with another chuckle. "We aren't kids anymore."

I shrug. "Hey, I just learned some creeper has been watching everything I do, like, all the time. I'm down to turn on the lava lamp and pull out a sleeping bag."

The curtains are already closed, but Zoe double checks them and the door. We make popcorn, turn on The Mummy, and lay out sleeping bags on the floor.

It's going to be a long night.

Deep breaths. I inhale, rubbing my sweaty palms on my pants. Zoe glances over at me from the passenger seat.

"You okay?"

"It's debatable. I'm glad we finally found this asshole. I'm also terrified by what we're going to find inside his apartment."

"Welp." Zoe points a finger at a blue sedan on the far end of the parking lot. "We don't have to worry about finding *him,* so that's a plus."

It's Friday morning. Last night, I slept maybe a total of ten minutes. The description of Reggie camped out in the bushes watching my every move from our living room window freaked me out beyond anything a horror movie could do. Even a sleepover in the living room didn't help.

I nod, eyes fixed on Reggie as he strides towards his car. I hunch down in the seat. We took Zoe's car to avoid being recognized. Still, I practically melt into the faux leather as the sedan rolls by.

"Clear," Zoe says. "Let's do this."

We hurry out of the car and dash up the outer set of stairs. The complex is nice. It feels homey like ours but probably with more college students. As Zoe told me earlier, it makes sense to find a spot where coming in and out at odd hours won't be noticed.

Still, we pass a few little scooters, one dump truck toy, and some potted plants as we make our way down the outer balcony toward Reggie's door.

"Right." I rub my hands together, glancing in both directions before inching toward the door. I've got my usual black on, but I went a bit further into ninja mode. A scarf covers the lower half of my face, and I've got on a pair of lace gloves to avoid leaving fingerprints. "You know how to pick a lock?"

I catch Zoe's look of utter disgust as I turn to glance at her.

"What?"

She gestures, looking like she's about to vomit, at a little rock beside a somewhat scraggly potted plant. "He's got a fucking hide-a-key. Amateur."

I snort, bend, and pluck the plastic rock from the ground. Sure enough, there's a little switch at the bottom and a compartment opens with a key inside. "Are you more mad that he's a menace to our lives, or that he's making serial killers, and therefore you, look bad by being so utterly careless?"

Zoe scowls at me. "Yes."

I cackle and unlock the door.

This is the point where my courage ends. The door swings open without a sound, but my mind reads the whole scene like a horror movie.

"What if we find, like, bodies in there?" I whisper.

"Then he's even worse than I thought, which honestly doesn't seem possible." Zoe strides forward, no ounce of fear as she steps across the threshold.

I follow her.

The front of the apartment is normal. Well, normal-ish. The living room is sparse. A computer screen serves as the TV, set against the far wall on a rickety foldable dinner table. The walls are bare, the only furniture a set of outdoor patio chairs.

The layout is similar to ours, though the hall leading to other rooms is wider than the one we have. The kitchen is a mess. Zoe gags as she steps onto the brown stained linoleum and looks at the sink.

"Nope." She wheels and strides back out. "If we need to search the kitchen, I'm not doing it."

I nod, sticking my head in just enough to see a stack of dirty dishes, an overflowing trash can, and several questionable stains on the stove. "How can you both be serial killers and yet be so different?"

She doesn't answer. Instead, she walks down the hallway. I scurry after her.

The apartment is a one bedroom. The bathroom is as gross as the kitchen. Zoe doesn't even step a foot inside.

The bedroom, however, is surprisingly clean. A twin bed is shoved against a far wall, a crate serving as the bedside table. The dresser is stained but clear of clutter.

I move into the center of the space. "What exactly are we looking..."

The final part of my question dies in my throat as I complete my turn and face the open walk-in closet.

Zoe must read the absolute horror that floods my system. I'm frozen, fear dominating the fight or flight or freeze instinct as I stare at the murder board pinned to the back of the empty walk-in closet.

It's not like Zack's murder board. There are no red strings, no cute little sticky notes in Zoe's neat scrawl, no politely blurred images.

"Kar, this is it," Zoe breathes. "This is what we needed."

I nod, the ice in my veins thawed by her voice. "This is..."

"Absolutely nuts, yeah."

Reggie's murder board is a list. To the left are images of me. Well, me and men. Some are ones I've posted on socials, some were clearly taken without my knowledge. Me on a surfboard with Logan behind me holding my waist. Me tossing a handful of biodegradable confetti in the air as David stares at me instead of the bride. Me holding Marcus's hand as we leave Zoe's parents' house. Me kissing Connor after dinner with Zoe and Zack.

Each of the images lines up to one on the right of just the men. Each of those has a red X slashed through it.

My stomach rolls.

"Don't throw up," Zoe mutters as she leans in to study the board.

"Not going to," I say through gritted teeth, though that might not be entirely true.

Because at the top of the list, right above Connor, is a picture of me and Zack. His arms are locked around me, our lips pressed together, the river behind us. It's honestly a great photo.

And it sends fear through every inch of me.

"We have to…" I can barely breathe. I turn to Zoe, frantic. "Zoe, we have to…"

"Already on it," she says. I focus.

Her phone is in her hand, she clicks the screen and puts it on speaker. It rings once before: "Zoe?"

I nearly collapse with relief at Zack's confused voice.

"Is everything okay?" he asks.

"Yep." Zoe looks at me, her eyes wide. "Everything is great; just checking in. Cool if we come by in an hour or so?"

"Yeah, I've got some good info I found this morning. Hey, is Karrie okay?"

"As okay as possible," she says doubtfully.

I'm pretty sure I look like a Victorian ghost at this point, but hearing Zack's voice has at least brought some of the feeling back to my limbs.

"See you guys soon." Zack barely finishes his sentence before Zoe hangs up.

"What are we going to do?" I ask, breathing deep through my nose. The air is stale, but the oxygen brings thought to my brain where it wasn't before.

"We stick to the plan," Zoe growls. She gestures further to the right. Beside the *X*-ed out images of the men Reggie has killed are a set of pictures of the men Zoe has taken care of. Instead of *X*-es, most of these have question marks. Only Derek and Vincent are crossed out.

"You have something like this?" I ask in a hoarse voice. "Like trinkets or body parts or something?"

There's a long pause. I look up to see Zoe staring at me with incredulity on her face. Actually, she looks more offended.

"What?"

"No, I do *not* have trinkets. No, I do *not* have a creepy murder board. Know why?"

"Because you're not a slopp–"

"Because I'm not a sloppy idiot!"

Her frustration breaks through the horror around us long enough for a chuckle to escape my lips.

"So, how are we pinning everything on him?" I gesture to the board. "Besides this."

"Wait." Zoe squints at me. "Do you still have the movie stub from your date with Derek?"

"Yeah, it's in my... ohhh." My eyes go wide. There is a shoe box in my closet. It sits above my dresses, right next to my basket of gloves. And it is full of evidence of every date I've ever been on. From movie stubs to restaurant matchboxes to receipts. "Zoe, that's perfect."

She nods. "I know."

"Okay, so we go get that, take out a few things and wipe off my prints—"

"And bring it back here to stick next to this disaster of overt evidence," Zoe finishes.

I nod slowly. "This could work, Zoe."

"It will work."

I grin despite the stomach churning guilt that has begun to creep in. "Okay, let's go."

We both turn around and release matching little gasps. The closet door has swung part way closed and made a new set of trauma visible.

"Well, fuck."

"You said it," I murmur.

The door is covered in pictures. Some are normal-looking drivers license photos, cheerful group pics, a few selfies... the rest are bodies.

My mouth fills with metallic tasting spit. I gag.

"Don't," Zoe says.

"Zoe, they all..." I swallow, taking in the women before us.

"They're all you, yeah." Her voice shakes, this finally breaking the calm and collected badass she's been the whole time.

There are maybe half a dozen women pasted to the door. Each one has the same black hair, same fishnet/ripped jean style I love, same black or blood red or cheetah print painted nails.

"He's been trying to find someone to replace you," Zoe says. She gestures limply to the door. "None of them worked out."

"This is..." I close my eyes, breathing hard as I bend at the waist and put my hands on my knees. "This is too much, Zoe."

"Yeah, this is fucked. We sure we only want to get him caught? I'm thinking this guy deserves worse than jail time."

"No," I snap. "We need to clear you of all this shit." I wave a hand around the closet, still staring at the dirty carpet. "If Reggie ends up murdered or disappeared, that won't fix that problem."

There's a long pause before a grudging "fine."

My relief is short-lived as I brace myself before straightening. I force myself to look at the women on the door. The women Reggie murdered because of me for whatever reason. Maybe they turned him down, maybe he dated them, and he found they weren't similar enough to me. Maybe he just likes killing them.

I glance back at the murder board of men. "What are the odds that the first guy I ever went on a date with and my best friend are both serial killers?"

Zoe cocks her head as she nudges the door open with her elbow. "Well, originally, I thought the odds had to be somewhere past astronomical. But I looked it up, and considering that about one in twenty-five people is a sociopath, and taking into account the number of people you've dated, it stands to reason you'd double up. Though, I'd argue that this guy is a psychopath."

"There's a difference?" I groan as I follow her down the hall and into the living room.

"Yep. Me and Sherlock Holmes are sociopaths. Dexter and this asshole are psychopaths."

"Got it. Now, get me the fuck out of here before I wretch all over this disgusting carpet."

I skid into our apartment parking lot barely ten minutes later. Zoe slides across the console and takes the wheel while I book it upstairs. She's going to Zack's. Neither of us is okay with him being alone at the moment, reassuring phone call or not.

It's a business day, and based on Zoe's research, Reggie is a dedicated bank teller. There should be plenty of time between now and when he gets off work for me to stash a box of knick knacks in his death closet.

I fumble with my keys, but manage the lock and swing the door open. My fingers brush the bracelet on the wall, but I don't take my shoes off. Zoe can be mad at me later. I'm not taking the time right now.

I dash to my room, grab the box, and dump it onto the kitchen counter. There are a handful of things from amicable splits, dates that just didn't work out, one-nighters that were fun but nothing to write home about. I cut those from the rest, take a cloth to the box, and dump the rest back in.

I tuck the box under my arm, sprint back to the door, and make sure to double check the lock before I hurry to my car.

I'm halfway to Reggie's when my phone rings. It's Zoe. I plug in an earpiece and hit the green button.

"I'm almost—"

"Zack's gone, Karrie."

I hit the brakes. My heart slams against my ribs. "What do you mean?"

"I mean he's gone. The studio is a wreck. I think... I think Sloppy got him."

No, no, no, no... My mouth is dry, palms sweaty, and breath unsteady.

"I'm on my way."

CHAPTER SIXTEEN

TIPS AND TOKENS

It was already obvious that when we saw Reggie leave his place, he headed straight here. The absolute mess is a dead give away. TCT's meticulous notes are strewn everywhere, his murder board is knocked sideways, and his laptop is open and face-down on the floor. It's clear Tom put up quite the fight. But the linchpin is the recording that had been in progress, which is now playing on a loop of the moment Sloppy kidnapped him.

I am crouched just inside the front door to make sure I don't disturb anything as I listen to Tom do his movie trailer voice to introduce his topic for the session, only to be interrupted by the loud bang of the door getting thrown open. Reggie didn't even knock, the impolite bastard. But TCT didn't lock his door, so...

"Who the hell—" Tom's voice cuts off, and you can hear a shuffling sound.

"You're coming with me, pretty boy." Sloppy's voice manages to be menacing, and I hear the edge, the underlying desire to hurt someone in his tone.

"Wait, you're Reginald, right?"

Props to Tom for not sounding freaked out in the slightest.

"Don't call me that," Sloppy snaps.

"Mr. Stevens, then?"

Okay, Tom, you're joking with a serial killer. And this one is genuinely scary because he's unpredictable. But then I realize it's probably because he knows he's still recording. He's giving us a clue.

Because he's a genius, that shithead.

There's the sound of the scuffle that took place—the thunk of someone's body against the murder board and Zack's voice crying out in pain. The clatter as the board crashes to the floor. Papers flying, some grunting, the laptop going down. I can tell that's what it is because the microphone makes a loud *thwap* as it gets pulled down too. It's still plugged into the laptop.

And then the recording starts over. I'm guessing it's because of how the computer landed. Some button is being held down, playing the scene endlessly.

By my estimations, they have a thirty minute head start on us. Who knows what Sloppy could have done to Tom in that time, but I don't move because I know Karrie will be here any minute, and I promised not to do anything without her. Even if our next step ends up being the last one I want to take.

We probably have to enlist law enforcement, which makes my skin crawl just to consider it. Not just because it jeopardizes our whole framing operation, but also because they don't seem to be the most competent when it comes to... much of anything.

Karrie's loud footsteps give her away before she opens the door, so I move away to avoid getting hit when she flings it open in true theatrical Karrie fashion.

Fear and panic mingle in the depths of her gaze, magnifying the already wide-eyed expression she wears. Her hands go to her mouth as she takes in the chaos of the studio.

"Oh my God." She jerks, stepping forward as if pulled by an invisible string. "We have to—"

I grab her by the sleeve before she can move further into the evidence. "We have to be careful."

She meets my intense gaze, then nods, tears sparkling for a moment until she looks away. "What do we do?"

I click my teeth together a couple of times. "I want to check back at Sloppy's place. First to see if he's taken Tom back there, but also so we can plant the tokens."

Karrie's brows draw low over her eyes like everything I've said was in Japanese.

"The evidence to frame Sloppy?" I remind her.

She blinks, understanding dawning. "Right."

"Two birds." I shrug. "And we have to do that ASAP because I'm calling in reinforcements."

"Reinforcements?" she squeaks. "Like a murder posse? Oh my God, please don't tell me the reason you have no other friends is because they're all actually serial killers, and you've been protecting me all this time."

I roll my eyes. "Ew. Don't be ridiculous. I mean the police."

"Oh."

The recording starts over, and Karrie grimaces.

"Can we turn that off?"

I shake my head. "We have to leave it so the police have something to lead them to Sloppy."

She nods numbly and swallows hard.

I gently nudge her toward the door, but something tugs me back. A nagging little feeling in the back of my mind. Twisting to peruse the mess again, it hits me. TCT said he'd found something interesting, and I can't just leave if there's a clue that could help us in some way.

I step carefully around the room, holding my hand out to Karrie to keep her there as my eyes scan everything on the floor.

"What are you doing?" Karrie hisses.

I hold my hand up because I see it—TCT's notebook that has been entirely dedicated to the investigation into Karrie's dating history. It's buried under a few file folders that are spilling their guts out across the floor. It's not the neat, color-coded handwriting that catches my eye. It's the hastily scrawled and thrice circled note he jotted down in a margin—very unlike him. I snatch the notebook and head for the door, shooing Karrie out ahead of me.

I rush down the stairs with a giddy thrill shooting through me. Because I just *know* this is something important.

I beat Karrie to her car, opting to jump in with her and leave my vehicle at TCT's studio. Neither of us has to verbally communicate that's what's happening or that's it the best course of action. We just do it automatically.

My first thought is to dig in on the note TCT left for us, but I know I've gotta tag the authorities in first. If we want to look entirely innocent, I'm going to have to lead them to TCT's studio first because logic dictates that we wouldn't know about Sloppy's place. And we need the time to plant the knick knacks to frame him.

We pull up to Sloppy's apartment just as I hang up with the police. First of all, they didn't seem to be in any rush to get to the studio. But, second of all, they seemed rather skeptical about my reason for leaving the scene.

"Hearing" an argument and scuffle from outside isn't initially convincing, but they agree to "check it out." Which is code for "we'll head over when it's convenient for us."

I slam my phone back into my purse and look over at Karrie.

Her hands are twisting the steering wheel so hard, it's gotta be hurting her palms. But she doesn't seem bothered as she stares out the windshield at the apartment building.

I scan the parking lot for the blue sedan and decide that I'm not relieved when I don't find it. Not that I want Karrie here when there's a showdown with a serial killer who's obsessed with her. But because it means he's likely not here with Tom, which then means we don't know where he's taken him.

It feels like ants are crawling under my skin, and I can't imagine what Karrie must be feeling.

"What are we waiting for?" she asks, her voice wound so tight, it sounds painful for her to speak.

"I don't think he's here." I nibble my lip, then grip the notebook in my hand, looking down at TCT's color-coded notes. He has a list of license plate numbers and names attached to them, and I realize he's been tracking down blue sedans in the area.

That genius sonofabitch made the connection. But how much did he figure out?

"We need to get these knick knacks inside," I say, shoving my door open.

Karrie scrambles to follow suit, her shoulders hunched as she trails behind me toward the apartment.

I tuck the notebook under my arm as we walk up the stairs and go straight for the hide-a-key.

Karrie takes a tremulous breath when I open the door to reveal that Sloppy and Tom really aren't here, confirming my suspicion.

"Hurry," I urge. "And don't touch anything."

She nods, a determined set to her mouth.

I pull the notebook out while I wait, scanning the list of license plates and names when my eyes fall on the name *Reginald Stevens* with an arrow and *Karrie?* written next to it.

Under that is a string of numbers followed by the word *Lake*, and I tilt my head considering. It's the three-times circled note he'd made. I can see how hard he was pressing the pen tip down and know this must be what he'd wanted to share with us.

Below that is another scribbled question: *Buries bodies?*

Buries bodies? As in, the missing men?

"It's an address," I whisper to no one, fumbling for my phone to look it up.

Of course there are multiple options for a 28754 Lake. There's Boulevard, Lane, Circle, and Drive.

"Bingo," I breathe when the Lake Drive address shows me a fairly remote location surrounded by farmland.

"Bingo?" Karrie asks breathlessly as she rejoins me.

"I think I know where Sloppy took Tom. It's across the border into Idaho."

"We have to go!" She rushes out the door, leaving me to chase after her.

"We need to figure out how to get the cops there too. That was the whole point." At least we know the recording will bring them to his apartment to find the trinkets.

She shakes her head, black, red, and purple tresses cascading back and forth across her back. "They got Reggie's name from the recording. They'll look him up and find whatever you've found, right?"

I wince, not putting much stock in that. "I didn't find the address in my search. Tom did. It would take too long if we let the police figure it out themselves. But I don't know how I'll convince them to come."

She stops so suddenly that I run into her, and then she turns to me, her expression so intense, it's shocking. "What about the local police? In Idaho?"

It's one of those rare moments when I genuinely don't know what to do. "What would I say?"

"You'll think of something!"

I've never heard her quite so close to hysterics before, and I raise a brow.

She takes a cleansing breath and reins it in a little, a visible process that actually makes me realize how tense *I* am.

"You always do."

Her confidence in my abilities is admirable. But I've got nothing. If I call the police at Tom's studio with the info we have, we could get in trouble for tampering with evidence. Not to mention, they'll want us to come back for questioning, and we don't have that kind of time. There's no guarantee they'll take the address seriously either. I have no proof whatsoever.

Karrie's face is getting more and more intense the longer I ruminate on our options. Her dark eyes bounce between mine, and I feel the heat of her gaze like a laser. I'm worried she's going to start shaking me to knock some ideas loose.

Then it hits me, and I gasp. "Anonymous tip!"

She claps her hands. "Anonymous tip!" With a questioning tilt to her head, she repeats, "Anonymous tip?"

I've already got my phone out and type as I speak. "I'll pretend to be a passerby who spotted a suspicious character dragging a man's body into the house."

She nods and starts pacing, wringing her hands like a wet washcloth.

And because I can multitask like a boss, I give my strategic anonymous tip while watching Karrie as she stops pacing, her thoughts putting a very intense emotion on her face that I can't discern.

She lifts her phone, typing furiously, and there's a determined set to her jaw when I hang up the phone. "Did they take the tip seriously?"

I wince. "Hard to say. It takes about forty minutes to get to this cabin from here."

She nods and licks her lips, looking at the map she's pulled up on her phone. "I bet I can get us there in thirty."

An excited tingle rockets through me. Looks like I'm going to get my show down with this life-ruining asshole after all.

I grin. "Then do it. When we get closer, I can call the local precinct and report a break-in or something. Hopefully, that will get them there fast enough."

Her answer comes in the form of her spinning on her heel and running to the driver's side of her car. She doesn't even wait for me to finish buckling before she's peeling out of the parking lot.

A Dark and Stormy Night

It's the wrong time of day for this. The shining sun, puffy white clouds, wind blowing through the trees as we zoom down the highway. I'm pushing ninety with the windows down. My phone is hooked to the holder in the air vent, the GPS a bit behind my speed as it continuously changes the estimated time of arrival.

Fear has a stranglehold on me. I know Zoe can see it. She keeps glancing in my direction, worry in her gaze.

Reggie. Fucking emo Reggie from freshman year. The kid asked me to the fair. I barely remember the date. There was an incident with the guy manning the ring toss; Reggie got mad about not making his shot and threw a bit of a fit.

I'd already not been enjoying myself, but that was the last straw for me.

Zoe was close by, as usual. I made sure we ran into her, gave the signal for her to claim a family emergency, and left early.

Rage begins to overtake the fear. Rage for every fucking douchebag who thinks he owns a woman after one date. Rage and a bit more understanding about every man Zoe killed for me. Her list, the reasons behind them—I get it. Now more than ever.

My hands are steady on the wheel. Ahead of us, roiling gray and black clouds overtake the blue skyline. The road is surprisingly empty, but I suppose it tracks as we are in the middle of nowhere at this point.

It's too quiet.

"Music, please." I glance at Zoe. I'd normally turn something on myself, but at this speed, it's safer for her to do it. Besides, if we die in a fiery car crash, who is going to save Zack? My faith in the local law enforcement matches Zoe's.

With twenty minutes to go, Zoe plugs into the AUX and roaring metalhead music blasts through my speakers. My breath steadies, heartbeat finally slowing as the bass reverberates in my bones.

We drive into a storm. The wind slams through the trees as I shut off the music, roll up the windows, and double check that my lights are off. The turn-off from the highway is a quarter-mile away. The sky grows dark, and it feels fitting for the mood.

I slow on the gravel but am still going fast enough that rocks are flying into the undercarriage and dinking the metal.

"Slow down when we get close," Zoe murmurs.

I nod, both hands on the wheel, eyes fixed as far ahead as I can see. More trees clutter the sides of the road. A few turn-offs make me worried we will miss our stop, but another look at the GPS shows I'm still on course.

As we get a mile out, Zoe unplugs from the AUX and dials 911 again. Her acting is phenomenal as she breathlessly and tearfully tells the operator someone is breaking into her home. She gives the address, then rolls her eyes at me before hanging up and turning off her phone.

"How long?" I ask through clenched teeth.

"She said the nearest car is a good twenty minutes out, minimum. Wanted me to stay on the phone with her and hide in the closet."

I flex my fingers around the steering wheel. My nose wrinkles as a foul stench filters through the vents. "What *is* that?"

Zoe cocks her head to the side and gets a thoughtful expression. "Pig farm."

I raise an eyebrow. There will be time to ask how she knows that later. For now, I slow as we get to the very end of this dirt road. A house sits in the distance, surrounded by towering evergreens. I veer off the drive, steering the car through some tall grass and coming to a stop a good hundred yards from the building with a cluster of smaller trees between us.

"Nice," Zoe murmurs.

"Can't let him see us coming." I swallow. "Do you think..." My voice catches, stomach rolling as unwelcome thoughts sneak into the forefront of my mind. "Do you think Zack is still–"

"We've got nothing to prove he's dead," Zoe cuts me off with a hard look. "We run under the assumption he's alive until proven otherwise."

I nod, my throat too tight to speak.

"Okay." Zoe heaves a sigh. "I knew this day would come, but I was hoping to avoid it as long as possible." She gives me a look like she's about to ask for a gyno exam. "I need to borrow one of your sweatshirts."

I blink, startled out of my fear for a second. "What?"

"Look at me!" Zoe hisses. She gestures to the pale blue jeans and soft pink top with little white dots. "I don't exactly scream covert mission. I need something black. I know you have a collection of hoodies sitting in your back seat."

I stifle my chuckle at her pained expression. "Uh, yeah." I open the door and hold up two options. I—unlike my bestie—am already wearing nothing but black. I even pull out my scarf from where I'd tossed it when I got too hot on the drive.

Zoe inhales and pulls on the long black sweatshirt. It's disturbing to see her wear something so dark. I think the last time she wore black was at her grandma's funeral a decade ago. Even then, she'd had a pink ribbon in her hair.

"Saving Zack?"

I suck in a breath as well, my gaze darting to the road where—hopefully—the cops will pull up soon. A rush of fear goes through me at Zoe's use of Zack's name. Her not calling him Tom slams the reality of what we are doing into my brain.

"Saving Zack," I agree. "Let's go."

We dart around the edges of the trees. Massive root systems and thick trunks get as close as ten feet from the cabin. It's the only reason I'm glad it's not dark yet. That's a tripping hazard to the max.

As we get closer, it's clear the building is small, maybe two rooms at the most. From the gear strapped to the side wall, I gather it's some kind of hunting or fishing place.

A light hangs from the front porch, but it's not lit. The front also has two small windows, the blinds pulled on both. We crouch, stepping as quickly and quietly as possible as we circle the house. The sides are windowless, but the back has a double set of small windows matching the front. They're maybe 2x2.

"Hang on," Zoe whispers, tugging my sleeve. She snakes forward.

I follow, my breath cold in my lungs as the wind whips at our clothes. Overhead, thunder cracks, making me jump. A light drizzle of rain begins to fall.

We get to the bottom of the window, me standing straight while Zoe ducks to avoid the top of her head being visible from within. We exchange a glance and look in the window.

My mouth opens just as Zoe's palm slams into my lips, locking the gasp within. She gives me a meaningful glare, and I nod.

She shakes her head, removes her hand, and we both return to our view.

Zack is in the room. His back is to us, but I recognize the hair, the clothes, the shape of his shoulders. Besides, who the hell else would it be? He's tied to a wooden chair, thick ropes wrapped many times around his arms and legs. The pressure must be excruciating; I can see where the material is cutting into his forearms.

The room seems pretty bare. A bed with a comforter you'd expect in a log cabin—black and red checked—a small door that leads to a bathroom, and a larger door that appears to lead to the main room. I can make out the edge of the front door just beyond a russet leather couch.

"We have to—" I cut myself off, eyes going wide as a shape moves in the doorway beyond, and Zoe and I both duck.

The rain is still light, small dewy droplets settling onto my hair and clothes. But it's not loud enough to block the voices coming from within. I ignore my screaming muscles at maintaining my crouch to listen.

"You've got till tomorrow to change your mind, pretty boy. If I don't get what I want by then, you go the same way as the others."

My stomach lurches at the sound of Reggie's voice. It's different—would have to be—than I remember. Still, he had a strangeness to him when we were fourteen, and his voice gives me the heebie-jeebies just like it did back then.

"I'm not..."

I grab Zoe's arm, my fingers trembling at the weak cough that breaks Zack's sentence.

"I'm not helping you get to Karrie."

My heart slams against my chest, and tears pool in my eyes. Zoe's eyebrows are furrowed, her gaze fixed on a random point on the wall as she concentrates on listening.

"You'll tell me what I want to know, Zack." Reggie spits his name with malice. "The others got me close, but something is still off from what she wants. You're going to tell me what it is, whether you want to or not."

Zack screams.

Zoe is ready for me again, grabbing my shoulders and practically tackling me to stop me from jumping up to see what's going on.

"We can't—" I can barely breathe. "Zoe, we have to—"

"I know," she hisses.

She pushes me, and I let her move me away from the windows and around to the far side of the house.

I'm seeing spots. I lick my lips, my tongue dry as cardboard as I wring my hands together. "What do we do?"

"Well, we sure as fuck don't wait another—" she glances at the watch on her wrist—"fifteen minutes for the cops to get here."

I nod. Then I meet her eye. She's not going to like this.

"He wants me."

"That much has been pretty well established, yes." The dry humor in her voice tells me things aren't beyond hopeless. She still feels confident about our odds.

"So what if I—"

"No. No. Absolutely not. Not in a thousand years would I let you go into a house *alone* with a serial killer."

I can't decide which aspect of that to poke holes in, so I just raise an eyebrow at her and put my hand on my hip the way I do every time we argue about me doing something she doesn't approve of.

"This is our best shot. I distract; you get Zack. When you two are out, I'll stall for time till the cops arrive."

"Fuck no."

"*Zoe*," I snap. "We don't have time for this, you know that."

She grits her teeth and presses her lips together, her hands doing that clench thing again as though she can feel the hilt of a blade between her fingers. "I can't believe I didn't bring my attache."

I open my mouth, then close it again, completely befuddled.

"Nevermind," she says on a sigh. "Okay. You distract; I get Zack. But we aren't waiting for the cops. I'm not leaving you alone in there."

I nod and bite my lower lip as thoughts fly through my mind. "Maybe there's some kind of weapon in the room Zack's in?"

"Maybe."

"Reggie probably has something; maybe I can get it away from him."

Zoe closes her eyes for a beat. "Do not get close enough to take a weapon from him. Promise me."

I glower.

She narrows her eyes. "You just said we don't have time for this. Promise, or we don't do this plan at all."

"Fine. I'll keep my distance."

"And I'll find a way to get you out of there."

I nod.

We stare at each other for a long second and then fly into each other's arms.

"You know I love you, right?" I mutter into the locks of blonde hair hiding her ear.

"Murder and all?" she whispers. There's a rare vulnerability in her voice that nearly breaks my heart.

"Murder and all."

"I love you too."

We pull apart. I head around the front; she goes to the back.

I take the steps of the cabin with every bone in my body trembling. My throat is dry, my hands clammy, my stomach roiling. I'm also soaking wet.

Light seeps from the cracks in the door jamb and the gaps in the curtained windows. I inhale.

Images flash through my mind. A collection of beautiful and horrible things. Zoe and I as kids, trading those little elephant bracelets, making the promise to be best friends forever. Those kinds of promises don't usually last.

Vincent, his fury palpable, rage expelled as he pummeled me nearly unconscious.

Zoe's expression when she opened the door to find me leaning on the porch post, barely able to stand.

The two of us setting up new homes in various cities. An adventurous life. A free life. A life she kept safe in the form of sweater stains and buried bodies.

Zack, the nervous way he brushes a hand through his hair. The way he waits for me to answer his questions. The way his lips felt against mine.

My hands clench at my sides.

I exhale.

And open the door.

Reggie turns as the door swings open, little pelts of rain immediately dampening the hardwood floor.

"Ka—" He blinks, astonishment widening his eyes and causing the gun arm he'd been pointing at the door to go limp. "Karrie?"

My eyes twinkle in that practiced way I usually reserve for a night club. I force the edges of my mouth into a wide smile, raising my eyebrows like I've just seen the most wonderful surprise.

"Hey, Reggie."

CHAPTER EIGHTEEN

THE RING

*N**ope. Nope. Nope. Nope.*

The word reverberates like an anxiety-wrapped mantra in my mind as I watch Karrie stride with determination toward the front door. This plan is hasty, dangerous, and unpredictable. Three words I would never want associated with me or my methods. Especially when it comes to murder. Not that we're guaranteed a murder in this scenario, but a girl can hope.

There's no turning back now, though, so I creep around to what I assume is a bathroom window—it's the same size as all the other windows in this creepy hunting cabin. It's the only one that has that gauzy film people sometimes put on to keep prying eyes from looking in. Though I don't know who they'd think would sneak a look. This place is almost as remote as it gets.

Pig farm stench notwithstanding.

Now to see if the person who was so worried about Peeping Toms was as concerned about Sneaking-In Zoes.

I grit my teeth and pull up on the window. It makes a little crack sound like the moisture from the shower (because this damn thing opens into said shower—WTF?) has glued it shut. I wait a half second to listen for someone coming to investigate before I hoist myself up.

The bathroom is dark, so I can't see much, but the musty smell and Sloppy's house-keeping habits at his apartment are not giving me much hope for clean surfaces. But before I have to force back a gag, I hear Sloppy's shocked voice, which pulls my attention.

"Karrie?"

I'm counting on her being a really good distraction so I can slither head-first through the window like the girl from *The Ring*. I hold back some colorful curses when I land louder than I mean to on my hands. My legs slide through after, and I do a pseudo handstand that would've made my childhood gymnastics coach proud. I did not think the logistics of this situation through. If this were my rodeo, I would have obtained the blueprints for the place. But we hadn't had the time.

Hasty.

I huff a breath, lowering my legs carefully as I hear Karrie say, "Hey, Reggie."

And it. is. magic. She's tapped into patented Flirty Karrie mode despite the circumstances. Sliding on the bewitching persona, she could convince anyone that she'd rather spend all of her time staring into their eyes than be anywhere else. I've seen the spell it casts over people, and it is a thing to behold and something so incomprehensible, even a scientist like me cannot understand it. I've tried to study it.

It's just Karrie's special power.

Suppressing the threat of another gag as my hands slide across the basin of the shower, I crawl out of it and onto the sticky-feeling linoleum floor, reminding myself we are saving someone's life, and I can shower in bleach when we get home. I creep toward the door to the bedroom where I know TCT is tied up. His wide eyes are already locked onto my position when I peek out like he was expecting me to be there.

I hold up a finger to keep him from giving me away, making sure the finger doesn't get close enough to my mouth for germ transfer, though I still hold my breath just in case.

"How-how did you find this place?" Sloppy asks, his voice almost awed.

I count on Karrie's magic holding out and creep across the wood floor to Tom, my eyes catching on the torture implements lined up neatly on the bed a few feet away. Reaching for the ropes that hold Tom captive, I feel the fibers are slick with blood. Anger shoots fire through my veins unexpectedly, and I break a nail in the process of rage-untying (yes, that's a thing).

"You let Karrie take on this psycho?" Tom hisses at me, distracting me from listening to what Karrie says in response to Sloppy's question.

It's like someone poured water over hot coals, and my rage spits and hisses, especially as a second hot-pink fingernail cracks in the process of undoing the knots in the ropes.

"I am not in charge of Karrie, first of all," I whisper through gritted teeth because, of course, I hadn't *wanted* her to either, and it pisses me off that he thinks I would be okay with it. "And second of all, you ungrateful asshole, we're here to *save* you. So maybe try 'thank you' without the judgy pants."

He sucks in a breath. "I didn't mean—"

"Just shut up," I snap as the ropes fall away.

"It's been a long time."

My head shoots up at Karrie's purred words. I still hear the tremble buried in her voice though, and I know she won't be able to hold him off for long.

Tom makes a face like he just smelled the pig farm before he slides from the chair to the floor. I can't decide the best course of action. We can't leave Karrie alone, but we have an advantage that Sloppy Stalker doesn't know I'm here or that I've untied Tom.

But, as if my thoughts were telepathically planted in his brain, Sloppy seems to catch on to whatever Karrie is up to. He does have a brain after all (though its function is debatable) and probably realizes Karrie wouldn't actually show up here to see him. He already knows about her feelings for Tom.

"Quit messing with my head." His voice is low and sends a thrill of warning through me.

And, sure enough, he stomps over to the bedroom to check on Tom and finds us both crouched on the floor next to the chair, and aims his gun in our direction.

"I knew it," he says through his teeth. "Can't do anything without her best friend, Zoe."

His mocking tone rankles, and I regret not shanking him the night before when I followed him home. It would have been a mess to clean up, literally and figuratively, but he'd be dead, and we wouldn't have to figure things out now. Not to mention Tom wouldn't have gotten caught in the cross-fire.

I stand up slowly and give him a smug grin. "What's up, Reginald? Couldn't take a hint last time and thought you'd try again?"

Sloppy strides toward me, and I react just a half-second too late when he raises his hand, so he still catches me in a pistol-whip across my cheek. Not as hard as it would have been had I not jerked to the side, but it still leaves a stinging streak along my skin.

When I return my eyes to him, his chest is heaving as he glares at me.

And then a flash of movement in my periphery catches us both off-guard, and I stumbled backward when Tom tackles Reggie to the ground, sending his gun skittering across the floor. I immediately spin and sprint for it while Tom occupies Sloppy in a physical struggle that elicits grunts and curses. I'm not sure who's winning because my eyes are locked on that muted glint of metal across the room.

They roll into me from behind, and I squawk as it knocks me to my hands and knees. I don't spare them a look and crawl the rest of the way. The second my hand lands on the butt of the gun, a loud thud reverberates through the room, vibrating under me, and I gasp.

I spin, breathless, only to find Sloppy has already made it to his feet, and the fucker has another gun—a tiny sissy gun he probably pulled from his ankle or something. The barrel is only inches from my forehead. Blood is trickling from the corner of his mouth, so I know Tom at least got one good punch in.

My eyes shoot to his motionless form in the corner, and a thrill of fear sends ice through my gut. No. I can't let Tom die. I can't let that happen… to Karrie.

I refuse to acknowledge the cold, dark fissure that starts in my own heart at the very thought of losing him.

Sloppy runs the back of his hand across his mouth. "Keep getting in the way, you meddlesome bitch." Spittle and blood spray from his mouth, and I flinch away.

BLOODY HANDS

The second Reggie's attention turns from me, I make a mad dash toward the kitchenette. It's a small thing, basically part of the main room. But there is a row of kitchen knives stuck to a long magnetic strip on the wall above the stove.

My fingers latch around the largest—I assume a steak knife—and I yank it off the wall. Behind me, a thundering crash resounds, and it feels like it shakes the entire cabin.

Fear grips my heart like a vice, pain radiating through my ribs.

I stumble as I turn around, running back toward the doorway to the bedroom.

Zack is on the ground. Blood oozes from a slash in his forehead. Another pump of adrenaline-filled rage floods my system.

It's nothing compared to what I feel when I see Zoe and Reggie.

Zoe is kneeling, one hand gripping Reggie's gun, the other by her side as she stares at him with hatred in her gaze. Of course she doesn't look scared at all because it's her.

Reggie stands just inside the doorway, a smaller pistol in his hand, pointed straight at her head.

Buzzing fills my ears.

A single word breaks through the tumultuous storm of fear and panic and fury within me. It cuts into my mind like a shard of ice.

"*...bitch.*"

No one calls my best friend a bitch.

I lunge.

The sharp blade slides through the flesh at the curve where his shoulder meets his neck. He freezes, lurches. The knife catches on his collarbone as he sinks to his knees. I keep my grip on the hilt, a sickening slurp sounding as Reggie clears the edge of the blade.

Blood spurts from his jugular like a cherubic angel pissing in a fountain. It drips from the tip of the knife still clenched in my hand. It stains the wall and the floor and my hands and my clothes and...

I wheel around and vomit all over the back of the leather couch.

Scrambling sounds behind me cause fear to clutch my insides. I spin around as I wipe my mouth with the back of my hand, frantically waving the knife through the air.

"Whoa!" Zoe reels back, her hands shooting up as her eyes widen. She's managed to avoid stepping in Reggie's blood in the process of getting to me. An impressive feat given the amount of it coating the floor.

Zack's clothes are going to be ruined.

"Zack," I breathe, a renewed fear cutting across my nausea.

I shift to look at him, still somewhat numb. Zoe is at his side before I've taken half a step. Her fingers go under his neck and barely a second later, she looks at me with relief in her eyes.

"He's alive. Which is more than we can say for Sloppy."

A sob breaks from my lips. The knife falls from my grip, and I'd sink to my knees if the ground wasn't absolutely filthy. Instead, I take several steps backward, bumping against the kitchen counter as Zoe follows me.

"I killed someone," I half-whisper.

She nods solemnly. Is that disappointment on her face?

"I killed someone." Panic laces my voice. I take several deep breaths, my hands shaking as I take in the red staining my skin.

"Yes, and I've killed several people."

"*Zoe*," I snap, because as much as I'm glad Reggie is gone, I'm not okay with the amount of blood on my hands. Literally and figuratively.

"What? He was about to shoot me. You saved my life, Kar."

That helps. I nod slowly, my lips trembling as I exhale. "Right." I pause, thinking. "Is this what you feel about the idea of sex?"

Zoe does an eye twitch. "Probably. You've slept with way more people than I've killed. I find the entire enterprise absolutely abhorrent."

"That's about how I'm feeling right now." I shudder.

Zoe puts a hand on my shoulder. "We're going to get through this. Like we get through everything. Together."

"Together." I take another breath and the nerves finally start to settle. "Okay Miss Serial Killer Expert. What do we do now?"

CHAPTER TWENTY

THIS LITTLE PIGGIE

It's lamentable, really. A waste of an opportunity. The only time I could put the theory to the test, and I won't have time. Or the need.

It's clear my abject disappointment shows on my face because Karrie's expression shifts from her shock and disgust to confusion.

"I read a few years back that one of the best ways to get rid of a body was to dump it in a pig trough," I explain.

Her eyes go huge and round. "What the hell are you talking about?"

"You smelled it coming in, remember?"

Her mouth is partially open and the absolutely uncomprehending look on her face is almost comical. Actually, totally comical, but she has no capacity for understanding how I could find humor in the situation, and I keep my laugh on lock-down.

"It would be so easy to get rid of Sloppy. Just toss him in and walk away." I sigh longingly again. "The pigs eat the whole body, and there's no evidence left."

Her lip curls back. "That is insane."

My shoulders droop. "And a moot point. I can already hear the sirens."

She curls in on herself, tipping her head to the side. "The pigs will even eat their clothes?"

I suck in a breath, then the horror fills me to the brim. "Ugh, you're right. We'd have to strip him." I make a gagging sound without deciding to.

Karrie shakes her head. "I can't believe you have no compunctions about eviscerating a man, but seeing him naked makes you balk."

I wave that away, trying not to let images of that very thing infiltrate my mind, but it's too late, and I shudder.

"I do not understand you." Karrie says. "Or maybe I'm starting to, and that's the problem."

"Just help me arrange some things so it looks like you killed him in self defense." I gesture with my hands for her to follow me to the other side of the room. "You have to be over here."

The disgust distorts her pretty face at the thought of walking near Sloppy's dead body, though she steps carefully around the puddle of blood that haloes him. It's almost comical that she can barely stand to look in his direction considering she was the one who killed him. Never thought I'd be saying that.

I roll my eyes, though, and urge her to move faster. "They'll never believe you were defending yourself from behind him." Urgency electrifies my nerves because the sirens are getting louder.

"But I was defending you," she argues weakly.

"Unfortunately," I say, glancing toward the door. I can hear the tires on the dirt driveway. "I don't think that counts, though we are in Idaho. They run things a little differently."

She nods, keeping her eyes turned away from Sloppy. Luckily, she dropped the knife in a logical spot for what we want this to look like.

I run through scenarios in my head, thinking I need to maybe lead them to the assumption that she was defending herself without actually saying she was.

"They'll be here any minute." The words tumble out of my mouth in quick succession as the pressure of discovery weighs heavily on me. "Zack knocked the gun from his hand, but he pulled out another and had us both pinned. He was going to shoot you when you grabbed the knife from his weirdo torture collection."

Her breaths come in and out faster and faster. "His what collection?"

I jerk my head toward the bed where I'd spotted the various weapons in a neat little row. It's clear he'd been planning to work TCT over a bit.

"He came toward you." I speak deliberately and clearly, trying to get her to repeat after me.

She nods and does: "He came toward me."

"And you stabbed him."

"And I stabbed him."

"Good."

A groan from the corner of the room pulls our attention, and Karrie gasps, rushing over to Tom's side as he stirs. She doesn't even seem to realize she's stepping right into the puddle of congealing blood.

"Zack?" she murmurs as his eyes flutter.

"Karrie?" he croaks.

The sound of fists pounding on the door interrupts their little reunion, and my stomach drops down to my toes. I might have been pretty level-headed about the whole murder thing, but we don't have this frame job in the bag yet. And while I don't regret a single life I've taken, I am also human and don't particularly want to go to prison. Those places are not clean.

"Police!" a gruff voice shouts.

"Back here!" I holler back, hoping I'm not inviting my own downfall into this mess of a situation.

CHAPTER TWENTY-ONE

SECTION 19-202A

I've never seen Zoe this tense. Angry, yes. Annoyed, yes. But even when I take her to night clubs, and she curls into a ball on a barstool with a book and a glass of red, she's pretty relaxed.

At the moment, with a dozen feet and three cops between us, she looks like a taut band about to snap.

The lights are hurting my eyes. Flashing red and blue and white that I feel like they could have shut off after they figured out there was no danger anymore. Zack is lying in the back of an ambulance, another pair of cops chatting with him.

I've refused to leave the door to the vehicle. The thought that they might drive him away before I can tell him how relieved I am that he's still alive, before I can apologize for dragging him into all of this, terrifies me.

Besides that—and my concern for Zoe—I'm surprisingly calm. Maybe all the adrenaline burned out during the stabbing. Maybe my battery is so low I'm about to collapse, and I'll wake up freaking the fuck out again.

At the moment, I'm just glad everyone I care about is still alive.

"Sorry, what?" I blink and glance at the cute lady-cop who has just paused while writing something in her little notebook.

"Why did you lie during the call to the police?"

I shake my head, widening my eyes and pouring what I have left into forming tears. "We didn't think anyone would believe us. We've both—" I glance at Zoe, blinking just right to let one of the tears fall. I swipe it away with too much urgency, like I can't bear to cry during such an important moment— "had times in the past when we've called the police on violent men. I guess there was too much doubt that someone would show up."

The melt in this woman's face almost dredges up some guilt for the mostly-lie. She puts a hand on my shoulder, her hazel eyes boring into mine. "You did the right thing."

I nod, my focus catching on the conversation behind me.

"I don't…" Zack sounds so tired. "I don't remember. I saw Zoe coming through the window. Karrie was… I was worried; she was distracting him."

"So, what do you think?" I ask with a wobble in my voice. "Am I… am I going to get in trouble?"

The lady-cop, Sanderson, shakes her head with a sympathetic furrow in her brow. "This was self-defense, Miss Dunshire."

The man who had been questioning Zoe turns around and strides toward me, water from the now-stopped rain glistening in his mostly-gray hair. "Actually, it was defense of another."

I immediately focus on folding into myself to give more distance as I stare up at him. "What does that mean? Am I going to jail?"

He lets out a chuckle, oddly warm and deep, before going somber. "You saved your friend's life. And the two of you likely saved that boy—" he gestures to the interior of the ambulance— "a world of hurt. Besides, there's section19-202A to think about."

I blink up at him like he's speaking French. 'Cause he might as well be.

He inclines his head. "You were defending another. Your use of force was absolutely reasonable to any sane person. Not to mention I just got a call from my counterpart in Spokane. They raided this nutjob's apartment and found a mountain of evidence that would have gotten him a handful of life sentences.

I'm betting we spend a few weeks on paperwork, bring you all into the precinct a few times to record your statements, and then you can put this behind you."

I swallow and nod. The relief on my face isn't an act. "Thank you."

He reaches up to pat my shoulder, seems to think better of it, and leaves me to Sanderson.

"I only have a few more questions, then you can talk to your friend before we take him to the hospital."

"Thank you."

A moment later, I'm hoisting myself into the back of the ambulance and settling as gently as possible onto the edge of Zack's cot.

"How are you feeling?" I ask in a hushed tone. My throat is tight again, real tears burn at the edges of my eyes, and I can't help the guilt building within.

His mouth twitches up in half a grin. At least his eyes are focused. That must mean his concussion isn't as bad as it could be. Still, seeing the little white strip over the crack in his forehead where he hit the wall sends a stab of pained worry through my gut.

"Zack, I'm so—"

"Don't you dare say sorry," he interrupts, taking one of my hands in his. He winces, and I catch sight of already bloody gauze wrapped hurriedly around his upper arm.

"But this is—"

He grunts. "You're also not allowed to say this is your fault. Because it's not. This is—" he gives a weak chuckle—"part of the job when you make a living hunting down killers."

I can't help the laugh at that because I've listened to the Armchair Detective, and while he's damn good at investigations, this is definitely the most danger he's ever been in. Unless for some reason, he's been keeping the juiciest bits of his investigations secret.

"Okay." I smile. "I've got what *not* to say. Am I allowed to say I like you?"

The half grin on his face spreads into a full one. "Yes."

I cock my head, putting a finger on my chin like I'm deep in thought. "Am I allowed to remind you about a certain conversation we had a few months ago?"

He shifts, trying to prop himself up onto his elbows. "Yes."

I put a gentle hand on his shoulder and ease him back down. Leaning over him, my loose hair creates a curtain framing our faces in shadow. "Am I allowed to kiss you?"

"Please," he murmurs, his dark eyes fixed on my lips.

I press against him, mindful of the injuries but eager to feel the heat of him. It's a long kiss that warms me from the inside and chases away the dregs of fear that had lingered. We only break apart when one of the paramedics clears their throat very loudly right behind me.

I jerk up, blushing—not with embarrassment but excitement.

"I'm sorry, miss, but you can't ride in the ambulance."

I give half a shrug as I stand and wink at Zack. "No worries. I couldn't afford it anyway."

Zack lets out a bark of a laugh and then clutches his chest. "Don't be funny right now, Kar."

I turn to the paramedic, my grin sliding into a serious expression. "I can come to the hospital though, right? We can follow you guys and see him right away?"

"That'll be up to the ER room, but given his injuries, I doubt you'll have a problem. He might be a bit groggy for the next little while though. Might have some memory loss."

I give my thanks, then jump down from the back of the ambulance onto the gravel road, pebbles crunching beneath my feet. I cringe thinking about what else I might find in the tread of these boots later tonight. But I push it from my mind.

The lights have stopped. Most of the patrol cars are gone. A pair of folks who must be from the morgue carry a black body bag out of the cabin. My stomach churns, but there's nothing left to upchuck. Besides, I don't think my body has the energy to throw up at the moment anyway.

Zoe strides toward me. She's gotten rid of my sweatshirt sometime during the questioning. The pale pink somehow matches my exhausted but elated mood.

"Ready to go?" I ask, my voice about as chipper as it gets.

She shakes her head. "You're getting way too used to this murder thing."

I loop my arm in hers with a grin, and the two of us make our way to the car.

Chapter Twenty-Two

LICENSE RESCINDED

I thought I was disappointed about the pig trough thing. Like, seriously, how perfect would it have been to just toss Sloppy into the pig pen like literal slop and wait for him to become swine crap? I'm ignoring the naked man part for now because this was a literal dream body disposal plan. No evidence, no ties to us, all the framing set up. Walk away. Epic zoom-out, roll credits.

But not only do we not need to worry about evidence, we don't even have to tell some faked story about self-defense. All my forethought gone to waste because Idaho is much more into the "stand your ground" law than some of the other states I've lived in. Not that I'd know their legal system since we live in Washington, but still.

The cops heard us describe the scream Tom had let out when Sloppy had started cutting into him (that bastard), and it was like anything we said afterwards was gold. One of the cops even said we might get an award and a parade.

Pass on both for me, but Karrie has always been into trophies. She has a whole box of them in Sloppy's apartment to prove it.

"Stop pouting. It worked out in our favor, remember?"

I glance over at Karrie in the driver's seat. She's practically buzzing with anticipation. The fear and horror are gone, but she's still incredibly anxious about getting to TCT at the hospital they'd taken him to.

"Yeah, yeah. It's great." There is literally zero enthusiasm in my voice. And I frown and try to mentally pep myself up.

Because, for real, this whole thing wrapped up in one of those unrealistically huge, bright, and shiny bows you see on car commercials during the holidays. Like your favorite dessert on a silver platter that you get to keep.

But... I wanted to do my Zoe thing. I wanted to have a story, get that suspicious glare from a detective, put my acting skills to the test. I mean, I literally kept my murderous past from my best friend for over ten years, but I know her well enough to specifically design my subterfuge. This might have presented a challenge, and I love a good challenge.

And even though I hadn't put much stock in the authorities' ability to make connections, they'd found the link between Sloppy and the cabin pretty quickly. It's a hunting cabin used only a couple of times a year by his cousin. To be fair, they already had Sloppy and the address to link, whereas TCT had made the jump by methodically combing through the owners of blue sedans in the area.

I have to give TCT credit. The dude knows how to get to the bottom of things. To be fair, he isn't bogged down in the red tape and paperwork that comes with being in law enforcement, so I have to go a little easier on the guys in blue. But past experience is hard to ignore.

Karrie pulls into the parking lot of this dinky, rural hospital a little too quickly, and I consider rescinding her automatic rights to driving us places. At least until her adrenaline high has worn off.

Hindsight.

Karrie whips in her seat to look at me, her expression intense. "Okay, I need you to tell me for real."

I blink, thrown off. Then, because she doesn't elaborate, I try to read her mind. Hey, sometimes it works. But I have no lead-up context, and that's really all there is to the telepathy.

When I remain silent, she huffs a breath. "What is Zack's secret? I have to know, so there is literally nothing standing between me and him anymore."

I snort. "That's all? Well, fine. I was going to let him tell you when he was ready, but if this is seriously going to be a hang-up for you, I'll tell you."

Her hands twist in her lap in anticipation, and I can't imagine what she must be thinking it is. Obviously if I didn't kill him, it's literally nothing to worry about. But

I get her desire to remove all secrecy from her life. The one I'd kept was a doozy.

I shrug. "He's divorced."

Her brows drop low as she pulls back slightly. Definitely not what she expected. "Wait, what?"

"He got married super young and was divorced within a year. He's probably just embarrassed about it."

She blows out a breath and flops a hand. "That's it? I've dated plenty of divorced guys."

"I know," I say flatly.

"Well, if that's all, then what the hell are we waiting for?"

She practically leaps from the driver's side, and I roll my eyes as I get out. "Kar, hospitals are notoriously slow. He's probably barely made it to a room yet. We're going to be pacing a hall somewhere, so maybe ease back so we can kill some time?"

She shoots me a glare, and I hold up my hands in surrender.

It was worth a shot, however misguided. I have severely misjudged the depth of her feelings for Tom. I mean, sure, I could tell how important he'd become just because of how much *I* like him. But I realize her heart has taken a leap it hasn't for a very long time. And for once, I am okay with what waits for her at the bottom of that cliff.

Any dude who can knowingly joke with a serial killer who was clearly there to kidnap him gets an extra vote in my book. Plus, he managed to work in a clue in the recording. That's next level. And makes me wonder if he's been in this kind of situation before.

Karrie rushes to the front desk as soon as we're inside, peppering the woman behind it with questions while I curl in on myself. Who knows what kinds of germs have come through this place in the last few hours?

With the number of people sprinkled throughout the waiting room, I am debating about going back to wait in the car. But I want to be sure True Crime Tom is alright too.

We're buzzed through a set of double doors, and Karrie jogs down a maze of hallways that get me turned around, but she's frantically reading room numbers and following arrows with the determination of a hound on the scent of a fox.

I am in complete awe.

Our wet shoes squeak on the floor as we turn yet another corner, and Karrie skids to a stop.

"Zack!" she cries, rushing into the room, and I trail behind her.

He's already in a gown and has clearly been giving the nurse hell because she has her hands against his shoulder, and she wears a look of such exasperation that I'm wondering if she might sedate him in a minute.

"Karrie!" TCT says, his voice flush with relief. "I need you to get me out of here."

"We need to stitch this gash and monitor you," the nurse says through clenched teeth. "You clearly have a concussion."

"Which you can't do anything for anyway," he points out, his voice glinting with an edge I don't understand.

I realize belatedly that there's a sheen of sweat glistening on his forehead, and it becomes clear that it's because he's nervous as all get out. I looked deeply enough into his past to know there's no reason in his own medical history to be nervous about hospitals, but maybe it was someone else. His brother died when he was a teenager, so I wonder if that's it.

"So just stitch me, and let the pretty girls take me home."

The nurse turns to Karrie as if she might be able to talk sense into him.

Karrie lurches into action, a soothing smile on her face. "Let's start with that part. Clean and stitch him. Would you allow him to come home with us? We can keep an eye on him there?"

Um, what is this *we*? But because I am such a nice person, I offer what help I can in this scenario. "Legally they can't keep you here against your will." I fold my arms across my chest to keep from bumping or touching anything, even if the place smells like an antiseptic factory.

The nurse huffs a frustrated breath through her nose at my words, and I get a secret thrill of satisfaction at pissing her off.

"Fine," the nurse grits out, stomping out of the room to get the supplies she likely needs.

Karrie's hands gently cradle TCT's face, and I almost look away at the intimate moment I'm trespassing on.

"I'm so glad you're okay," Karrie says softly.

"Only because you—and Zoe—came to rescue me."

I glance over, and he's looking significantly at me, thanking without words. And, shit, what is this squeezy feeling in my chest?

"Zack." Karrie's voice holds the threat of tears, and I fight my instinct to rush over and comfort. It's not only my job any more. "It's over. We're... we're free."

"Free," he repeats blankly, and I remind myself he has a concussion, which he earned trying to save me from Sloppy. That squeezy thing happens again.

"Free to be together."

Karrie's words land, and his face transforms, a lightness that makes him almost unrecognizable from the beaten up, anxious man he was just a moment before.

I definitely shouldn't be here for this. But as I try to make a hasty exit, the nurse blocks me by coming back into the room with all the stitching accouterments glinting in the harsh fluorescent lighting, and I back up to let her through.

At least Karrie got TCT in a better mood for this whole process. The nurse should give her a lollipop or something.

"This shouldn't take long," the nurse says, her expression pinched. "And then you can take Mr. Lim home, against medical advice." This she adds very pointedly, dividing a look between all three of us.

"If you have some instructions or something about what to look out for, I can make sure I monitor the situation for any changes," Karrie offers, giving her a bright and friendly smile.

The nurse purses her lips, then sighs, heading back out of the room to get whatever that might be.

I click my tongue. "Pretty sure their version of 'monitoring' doesn't involve getting naked, Kar."

True Crime Tom's face actually flushes with embarrassment, but Karrie just laughs and pats his cheek gently in reassurance.

EPILOGUE OF LOVE

Three Weeks Later

The whirlwind romance Zack and I have experienced the past few weeks has only been broken up by the occasional interview about Armchair Detective and my own insistence that I do, in fact, need to maintain my job. I took several days off after what happened at Reggie's cousin's cabin, but money is nice and normal felt needed.

The money factor is actually not as big of a deal at the moment. Zack's whole packet he had me sign when I agreed to do an interview months ago included a compensation package. Royalties, basically, on a portion of his Black Widow project. Armchair Detective gained about half a million followers in the first three days after he posted the episode with actual audio of himself being kidnapped.

Zoe has put up with Zack's near constant presence at the apartment. Possibly because I'm keeping certain sounds to a minimum and conversation topics about those sounds to absolutely zero. Not just because she's friends with Zack—an oddity I've never had to account for while filling her in about my sex life—but because after stabbing a man in the neck, I think I finally get how grossed out she is by the whole concept of banging.

I think she might actually like having him over; the girl does love cooking. This way, she gets to experiment with new recipes and try them out on someone with a more adventurous palate.

"Are you sure?" Zack asks in a hushed tone, for the tenth time, as we undo our shoes and set them on the little rack.

"Yes. Now hush." I give him a meaningful look. I don't need him spoiling the surprise. We just finished picking out a little white kitten for Zoe. As many jokes as I make about her being a cat lady, I think it might be true. And you can't be a cat lady without any cats.

Besides, the one we picked will look absolutely adorable with a pink bow. We just have to wait a few weeks for it to get a bit older, then I'm planning a whole girl's night to give her to Zoe.

Zack chuckles and heads toward the kitchen to wash his hands and see if Zoe needs any help.

I straighten and my gaze catches on the bracelets dangling from their hooks on the wall. Two of them, one with little black elephants, one with pink. Right next to each other, where they belong.

I join Zack at the kitchen bar a minute later, sliding onto the stool beside him as we both watch Zoe dice veggies like a master chief.

"So," she says, "what's next for the Armchair Detective, or—" she cracks a grin— "as it should have been named: True Crime Tom?"

Zack sighs and stretches. "I'm not sure. There are a stack of cold cases in the studio. A mafia thing in Seattle, some boring cattle disappearances, one case all the way in Ontario..." He shrugs. "As long as there aren't any murders in the area anytime soon, I'm probably going to take a few weeks off before I decide what trail to follow."

"Well," Zoe scoops a handful of carrots off the cutting board and deposits them into a bowl, "as long as you're good to Karrie there won't be."

I freeze.

Zack chuckles.

Zoe tilts her head at him. "Because if you hurt her, I *will* kill you."

"Ha-ha," I force out, my heart pounding and my eyes trying to express the insanity of what she's doing. But she isn't looking at me. "That's super funny, Zoe."

Zack huffs out another chuckle, turning to raise an eyebrow at me. "What's up, Kar? She *is* being funny."

I bite my lip as Zack turns his gaze back to Zoe. Her expression is as deadpan as it gets. Without taking her eyes from Zack, she flips the knife through the air, catches it, and only looks down when she pulls a zucchini onto the cutting board and continues chopping.

Zack's breath catches. He looks at me, his dark eyes wide and calculating.

My mouth is dry. I force another giggle before looking at Zoe. "Hey, how do you feel about cats?"

Part Two Coming Soon

KISS OR KILL SNEAK PEEK

“It's like this feeling in my stomach.” Zoe uses a claw-like hand to gesture toward her abdomen. “It's like this clenching and wiggling, like snakes or something. It feels good and bad at the same time. I hate it.” She slams the steak knife down on the cutting board. The carrots wobble dangerously. “Leave it to a guy to make me feel nauseated.”

My eyes go wide. I turn away and pop the cork out of the wine bottle. “Ahh.” Aim for casual. If I go head-on she's going to close up like a clam. “Is it just when you see him? Or when you have to talk to him?”

“All the time!” Zoe says through her teeth.

I stifle a chuckle at the frustration in her voice. "Yep, sounds familiar."

"What?" The word lands hard and sharp, like she's already prepared to not like what I'm about to say.

I turn. "You're going to want a wine glass."

Her brow furrows suspiciously. "What are you talking about?"

"You like him, Zoe. Like... like like him."

Zoe's eyes get bigger than I've ever seen as alarm flashes across her face. She reaches toward the counter, slender fingers closing around the handle of the knife. She's not holding it like she's about to finish prepping dinner though. She's holding it like she just caught sight of a guy hitting his girlfriend.

"Woah." I throw my hands up. "What are you gonna do? Kill him?"

She looks slightly wild as she brandishes the blade. "Maybe!"

"Zoe." I set down the wine bottle and approach her slowly. She lowers the knife to her side, a startling amount of fear in her gaze. "This is not the appropriate response to a crush. Not everything is solved with murder."

She glares at me. "We literally have a list of things that have been solved with murder."

I roll my eyes. "You're having a full on Karrie style freak-out right now." I raise an eyebrow, suddenly struck with realization. "Is this what it looks like when I have a breakdown?"

"No." Zoe scowls, planting the knife back on the cutting board and pressing her palm to her chest. "You don't hold a knife during a breakdown. You hold a toilet bowl."

"Wow." A humorless chuckle jumps from my lips. "Okay, that feels mean."

A LOVE NOTE

Hey darling people who read past the last page of a book – you're awesome.

Now, for a list of folks *not* on Zoe's hit list...

Beta readers, Meredith and Danielle, thank you so much for such a quick turn over on this little murder story. Your input – as always – bumped things to the next level. We are honored by how much you enjoyed the story.

Husbands, Brandon and Lupe, thanks for the time to write, the love, and the support. You *do* have nicknames, but we promise they're nice.

From Cheyenne to Tracey: you're the Zoe to my Karrie every day of the week. I love you a ton and – though our friendship didn't start as early as theirs – you're one of my absolute favorite people in the world, and I would 100% murder for you. Thank you for writing this with me. Thank you for being as excited as I am for the next one.

From Tracey to Cheyenne: Shiny, my friend, what a joy it is to spend time with you and write together! This story never would have happened without you, and honestly, I wouldn't be doing half of what I am without your encouragement. How do I explain what you mean to me aside from the fact that I would definitely murder for you too? Haters better watch out.

Big shoutout to friends and family and fans! Your support and love and hype mean the world. And we absolutely do this because it's fun but also because of you all!

If you enjoyed this story please leave a review!

For more from each of us, visit chlyn.com and traceyb arski.com.

About the Authors

Tracey Barski and C.H. Lyn have eight published works between them, this being the first they've done together. They both live in Colorado Springs with husbands and two small children each. In the chaos, they make time to write books individually and together. They also take turns giving each other coffee and compliments and regularly laugh at the hilarity of their own jokes. Find each of them on Instagram, Facebook, and TikTok. Visit Tracey at traceybarski.com and C.H. at chlyn.com

www.ingramcontent.com/pod-product-compliance
Lightning Source LLC
Chambersburg PA
CBHW021127190726
48288CB00008B/2542